The
Alfred Book
of
Ghastly Tales

The Alfred Book of Ghastly Tales

EDITED WITH AN INTRODUCTION BY
ELLIE WOZNICA

WHITLOCK PUBLISHING
Alfred, NY

First Whitlock Publishing edition 2018

"Stereopticon, Shotgun, Blender" was first published in
Phantom Drift: A Journal of New Fabulism, Issue 4: Fall 2014.

Whitlock Publishing
Alfred, NY

ISBN: 978-1-943115-28-0

This book was set in Adobe Garamond Pro on 55# acid-free
paper that meets ANSI standards for archival quality.

ACKNOWLEDGMENTS

A huge thank you to Dr. Allen Grove for all of his guidance and support.

A special thank you to Laurie Lounsberry McFadden of the Alfred University Archives for all her help with Alfred history and photographs.

This anthology is dedicated to Matt Chabot. Thank you so much, Matt, for your unwavering support.

NOTE ON THE TEXT

COMPANION

You're walking down the sidewalk after eating dinner at Ade Dining Hall. It's dark and you're alone. The orange incandescence of the lamps is all that holds the darkness at bay. You pull your jacket tighter over your body, but not even that can stop the biting wind.

You can see your shadow strolling in front of you, almost as if to beckon you to chase it. As you approach the next lamp in the line, your shadow grows fainter and fainter.

What's that?

You see a dark figure in the corner of your eye. Your heart skips. You are being followed. How long has it been since you were alone? Were you ever truly alone? These thoughts vanish in an instant as you see your shadow swing around you. It was just your shadow.

Your pace doesn't falter, but your entire body feels the relief of knowing you were the figure. Yet, you feel the urge to look behind you. But something stops you. Not fear, but embarrassment. What if someone saw you whipping your head around out of paranoia?

You realize the foolishness of that thought. Still, you look behind you. It is a mere glance, a movement so small you can barely see the sidewalk behind you. But that is all you see. You were alone after all. You laugh at yourself. You're a college student now; you're too old for such childish fears. But you can't shake the feeling that you aren't alone. That someone or something is with you while you walk through the dark. A silent companion.

–JOSHUA BENHAM

TABLE OF CONTENTS

ILLUSTRATIONS

INTRODUCTION

OMPILED HERE ARE ghost stories written by Alfred University students and a few faculty members. The stories range in form and narrative style from Haley Ruffner's epistolary tale, "A Ghost's Guide to Manners," and Julie Barr's "Alchol Violation" to some third-person narratives with Mary J. Rutherford's "The Blowfly Man" and Anna Wiegman's "ERR." The stories also vary in time from the mid 19th century in Meghan Rahner's "The Mortician" to the present day with Sydney Dominick's "Lighten Up, Dude" and Catherine Donahue's "The Black Knight." Tori Pellegrino's "Parallel to the Past" dances between the two.

With all of their differences, the stories in this anthology are all linked by the shared landscape of Alfred, New York. Some are set on Alfred University's campus; Ava Hameister's "A Lesson in Biology" and Juliana Gray's "We Are Outnumbered by Their Dead" take place in the Science Center, Barger's "Health and Wellness" in South Hall, and Joshua Benham's "Why Should I Care Who Died?" in the Powell Campus Center. Meanwhile, others are set in the rural village and surrounding areas like Allen Grove's "Waste Not." Wherever they are set, the writers in this anthology are using the ghost story genre to tap into Alfred's haunted history.

The dead have been present in literature for as long as literature has existed, appearing in Horace Walpole's *The Castle of Otranto* (1764), William Shakespeare's *Hamlet*

(1601), and one of the first English texts, *Beowulf* (circa 1000); Samuel's ghost even makes an appearance in the Bible. The ghost story genre itself became extremely popular in the Victorian period. Some obvious reasons for the genre's prominence include relatively high literacy rates and decreasing costs for publishing and distributing literature. The popularity of the ghost story genre is also linked to the growing interest in paranormal activities including séances, mesmerism, and hypnotism, all of which were seriously studied by the Society for Psychical Research. The Victorian period saw the birth of photography that, thanks to long shutter speeds and the limits of the early technology, often transformed our world into one haunted by ghostly figures. Later in the century, the discovery of x-rays caused magazines and newspapers to be flooded with images of transparent flesh.

The short story itself is largely a product of the Victorian period because of the presence of more periodicals and places to publish works of short fiction. As a result, short fiction became a popular source of entertainment. A good ghost story could provide a family with an enjoyable evening's amusement.

As in the Victorian period, the works included in this anthology will define "ghost" broadly. Some will feature indisputably supernatural occurrences, while others can be explained away as the chimeras of a haunted mind.

THE VALLEY OF THE INSANE

Before the town of Alfred was officially created by the New York State Legislature in 1808, the area served as the hunting grounds for the Seneca people. The creek running through the valley, the Kanakadea (sometimes spelled Canacadea), received its name from their native language. Translated into

English, the word means, "where the heavens rest upon the earth." The name stems from the topography of the valley and the creek's relationship to it. However, local folklore states the creek's name is derived from the people who died in the valley. Legend says the Seneca dubbed the land "The Valley of the Insane," a place where they exiled insane members of their tribe to live amongst the deer and elk they hunted.

The Seventh Day Baptists, "many [of whom] were veterans of the War of 1812, and descendants of soldiers who had fought in the Revolution" ("History of Alfred, NY") are credited with settling the town in 1808 as well as founding the university itself in 1836. Since its first days, the little village (originally called Alfred Center) has made a name for itself, not because its annual festival to celebrate the Hot Dog that brings college students from all around Western New York to Alfred's secluded countryside, but because of its unique history.

When exiting New York State Route 21, before you reach the village of Alfred, you will pass through Alfred's second noteworthy settlement, Alfred Station (originally called Baker's Bridge). Although there is no longer an operational train station, when the Erie Railroad was first created in 1851, Alfred Station was not only a passenger line, but also a way for the community to export agricultural products such as livestock and cheese. Approximately three miles away from the station stood a water tower and a place for railroad workers and engineers to stay overnight. This stop was commonly referred to as "Tip Top," known for being the highest point of the Erie Railroad. The steep grade proved to be very trying for the steam engines of the time. However, the trains continued to make the trek, responsible for providing Alfredians with items ordered from the *Sears, Roebuck & Co. Catalog*, products that ranged from clothes and household products to entire barns and houses.

ALFRED'S HAUNTED BUILDINGS

South Hall was originally opened as the Alfred Central School that offered high school classes to all of the town's districts, but it now sits with its windows boarded, the building delapitated and rotting, home to many of Alfred's stray cats. The building state of decay that it made it the perfect setting for Pellegrino's "Parallel to the Past" and Susanna Barger's "Health and Wellness."

A product of its time, Alfred University's classrooms and residence halls were illuminated by candlelight or oil lamps before electricity, and unfortunately, the iconic building, "The Brick," is one of its most well-known victims of fire. When The Brick was first built in 1858, it was even more impressive than it is now, standing tall with four large stories. However, a fire broke out in one of the meeting rooms on the highest level costing the building its cupola and one full story, compressing it down to only three floors. In the time both before and after the fire, The Brick served many purposes, some even considered a little haunting. Not surprisingly, the building inspired a couple stories in this collection.

Before the residence halls became coeducational in 1970, The Brick was a women's hall where Alfred University's first president, William Colegrove Kenyon, strictly enforced the segregation of the sexes. President Kenyon was known for his rules and need for little sleep. During his term as president (from 1857 to 1865) students would see him walking around campus after curfew making rounds with his lantern in hand. Careful to avoid him seeing men enter The Brick via the front doors, the ladies of the upper stories developed a system which involved a basket and a password; once the password had been spoken, the basket was lowered and pulled back up with a man sitting inside it. The observant man he was, President Kenyon watched from afar and learned about the secret. After he recited the password, the basket was lowered, and he climbed in. After he recited the password, the basket was lowered, and he climbed in. It wasn't until the women saw the top of his bald head that they screamed, let go of the rope and sent the basket and the president down to the ground. President Kenyon was not wounded in the fall, but that night did mark the end of The Brick's basket-boy-retrieval-system.

During World War I and World War II, the United States Army contracted with Alfred University and The Brick housed the soldiers, serving as both barracks and infirmary. Near the end of the first World War came the spread of the insidious Spanish Flu in 1918, which ran rampant, killing 10% of the world's population including some of Alfred's own residents. At the time, Alfred University did not have an infirmary to treat students, so The Brick's military infirmary served that purpose. Unfortunately, a nurse, some soldiers, and some faculty died as a result of the influenza. Some students who have lived—and some who currently live—in The Brick have reported hearing people who cannot be seen, feeling as though someone has crawled into bed with them, and three students even talked to one of the ghosts on a Ouija Board. Ruffner's "Prowl" focuses on the building's spooky past, and Rahner's "The Mirror" taps into its interesting architecture.

Unlike The Brick, the Steinheim was never a residence hall, but it is still said to house a spirit. Now the Career Development Center, the Steinheim was originally owned by President Kenyon's widower, Professor Ida Kenyon who started its construction in 1876. The structure itself is built of rocks collected from neighboring farm fields. Cemented into the walls of the castle are "rock[s] collected from ice age debris, all from within three miles of campus" (Alfred University Archives). The president of Alfred University at the time of its construction, Jonathon Macomber Allen, purchased the unfinished castle from Professor Kenyon. President Allen completed it, inspired by the castles he had seen on a trip to Germany with his wife, Abigail. The Allens made the Steinheim into a natural history museum and a classroom, finishing the interior with many variations of wood from the region. The Steinheim was privately owned by the Allens until after Abigail's death in 1902.

In 1863, Jane Brooks was officially found guilty of poisoning the wife of her lover, making her the first female convicted of murder in Allegany County. President Allen visited her in Sing Sing Prison and paid three hundred dollars for her skeleton which later resided in the Steinheim and was affectionately nicknamed "Sally the Skeleton." Sally was used in student pranks, can be seen photographed with students in scrapbooks, and even makes an appearance in Hameister's "A Lesson in Biology." Though Sally's skeleton presideded in Steinheim, the staff at the Career Development Center believe it is the spirit of Abigail Allen herself who inhabits the castle since her ashes were at one time housed there. Presently, Abigail Allen has been accused of making the elevator move to which the receptionist replies, "Oh, Abby!"

The Black Knight

Alfred University's class of 1908 wrote in their yearbook that their "mascot [was] the statue from the top of the former history-room stove." After that, the statue of the Black Knight became a token, passing hands from the Class of 1910, to 1912 to 1914, and then to 1916, dubbed the "Black Knight of the Even Classes." The Class of 1923 envied the knight, and it soon became a battle of the classes, the odds against the evens. As a result, students hid the Black Knight from one another, everywhere from blouses and trousers, to burying him beside the creek. The Black Knight survived the battle but took quite the beating. He is pictured in the 1931 Kanakadea (Alfred University's yearbook), accompanied by the following poem:

> The Black Knight
> The Even classes proudly boast
> Of a mascot, brave,
> A relic of an old black stove,
> Long since in its grave.
>
> The Evens still are prone to laugh
> At our oddity,
> But we retain the part which means
> Supportability.
>
> This duel ownership was caused
> (Some perchance know not)
> Some years ago by a class fight –
> Each a portion got.
>
> Each Junior Class receives in stealth
> Trophy treasured.
> One a legless knight now guards;
> One a knightless leg.

In Jean McCord's article, "The Black Knight" (1977), she writes, "Ralph Rhodes, President of the Class of 1942, wrote to the Annual Fund Office: 'If you ever want the 'Black Knight' returned, please let me know. It was last seen on campus in the Fall of 1939. Ellis Drake, Dean of Men at the time, asked me to retire 'it'—which I did.'" Unfortunately, after being returned and standing proud in a glass case in the Powell Campus Center, the Black Knight was stolen in 2005 and has not been seen since. Both Pellegrino and Donahue imagine his reappearance in their stories.

Hidden away in rural western New York in the Valley of the Insane, a small college town is overrun by crows and deer. There are buildings with unexplainable mirrors, creepy paintings, and townspeople with ghostly pasts. Nine dead in The Brick, a murderer's skeleton, and a missing knight. It's time to prepare yourself. Turn on your reading lamp, sit down, and get ready to enter *The Alfred Book of Ghastly Tales...*

ELLIE WOZNICA, APRIL 2018
ALFRED, NY

Seventh Day Baptist Church, circa 1920.

Tip Top, circa 1920.

Train wreck in Alfred Station, June 14, 1897.

South Hall, completed in 1909.

Student Army Training Corps in front of the Brick, Fall 1918.

The Brick, circa 1910.

The Brick on fire, November 13, 1932.

President Kenyon and his wife, Ida, circa 1865.

President Allen and his wife, Abigail, circa 1885.

The Steinheim, under construction from 1876-1892.

Inside of the Steinheim as natural history museum, circa 1900.

The Science Center, circa 1970.

Bartlett Hall, 1932.

The Black Knight with Alfred University Class of 1908.

The Black Knight before his disappearance, mid-1980s.

King Alfred Statue, 1996.

NEEDLEWORK
ELLIE WOZNICA

MY MOTHER REFUSED to stay still. She paced around our motel room for a week chain-smoking American Spirits and impatiently waiting for the season to change in the cheap replica of Claude Monet's *Women in the Garden*. When she finally sat down on the bed beside me, she sounded like the worried mother from every 90s movie. She said it was time for us to have "one of those new starts." I wanted to roll my eyes, but she always was a bit of a cliché, and she needed me to be supportive. She explained she wanted a project, something to keep her mind off her failed marriage and the sound of ballpoint pens frantically scratching on dotted lines. Having been left vacant and rotting for the past forty years, the Wilson House met her needs perfectly. She said it even had a tunnel connecting the laundry room in the basement to the two-car garage out back.

"How cool is that, Annie?" she asked between inhales.

"Real cool." I was trying to be enthusiastic, but I was preoccupied thinking about the typical teenager-moving-to-a-new-town-things; like how I was going to take down my Joan Jett posters off my bedroom wall without ripping the edges,

1

and whether or not I would have to dial long distance in order to call the friends I was leaving behind.

My mother didn't seem to notice—or care—about my lack of interest. "It's a neat story actually. I guess the original owners didn't want to go outside in the snow to get to their horses, so they dug a tunnel connecting their house to the carriage house."

"So, they get a lot of snow here then?" I looked out the motel window and at the abandoned gas station with two plow attachments resting on cement blocks.

"Try not to be so pessimistic." She put out what was left of her cigarette in the black plastic ashtray.

"Isn't that creepy? Couldn't people sneak into the house?"

She put the stub of her cigarette back in the carton. "Don't be silly. It's not like the city." She chuckled. "And the villagers don't like to go into the tunnel anyway."

"Why not?"

"It's where Mrs. Wilson killed Mr. Wilson." She tucked the carton into her purse.

"Are you kidding?" I asked. I was definitely paying attention now.

"Nope, but you have to hand it to her, she was a resourceful woman."

* * *

The summer that we moved, I gathered research in the campus library. Mr. Wilson worked as a carpenter in his basement, and his wife was a simple woman of feminine talents. It was obvious once we entered the home that Mr. Wilson did not have much say in the décor of the rooms above his workshop, but Mrs. Wilson seemed well versed in the art of interior design. The den was open and stale, the couch was angled towards the red love seat, and each window was lined with a lace curtain that complemented the pale pink throw pillows. I did not see any traces of elegance in Mrs. Wilson's taste, and quickly made a remark about updating the tacky style and furniture as soon as we accumulated enough money to do so.

My mother on the other hand, disagreed completely saying that the decorating was so quaint and just what she wanted. "Just have to do some cleaning and renovating of the structure," she said. I wondered what HGTV show she had heard that from, but I liked seeing her happy again, so I didn't argue.

She insisted that we explore the workshop, but I didn't like the idea of going down to where Mr. Wilson built every coffin for the county before his death. She rolled her eyes at my nervousness and said that she would check it out soon with or without me. I ignored her and hoped that a night of sleep would bring her some sense. At the top of the stairs, she asked me to come and see the great character of the master bedroom, but I was tired and knew I would have a lot of work to do on my new bedroom. I kissed her on the cheek as we parted and took my bags to the room at the end of the hall.

It was much bigger than my previous space in our home in the New York City, but it lacked the common privileges that I had become accustomed to. Unlike the enormous windows on two walls with beautiful skyscraper views, this new room had only a very small window looking out over the pond in the backyard, making the room much darker than I was used to. Before moving in, my mother had mentioned that since the Wilsons had no children and very seldom had visitors, aside from the master, there were no other assigned bedrooms. Luckily, mother had found a portable twin bed in the linen closet. She rolled it into the second biggest room, thinking I would enjoy the extra space. She promised on the drive over to get me a big stationary bed once we had settled in and made some progress with the renovation.

Though it was definitely not what I was expecting, I enjoyed the clean slate of the room's walls and looked forward starting over for whatever it was worth. I placed my bags on the floor beside the wheels of my bed and took a moment to absorb my surroundings. I had seen some pictures prior to our arrival, but only of the rooms on the ground floor, almost as if the real estate agent wanted to get in and out as quickly as possible. There were framed embroideries arranged in patterns on each wall, and a sewing machine on a table in the corner that led me to believe that my new bedroom was originally Mrs. Wilson's sewing room. At first, this fact added some charm to my new room, and I envisioned a very cute old woman sewing some of the embroideries on the walls. It did not take me long, however, to remember Mrs. Wilson's story in The Alfred Sun and how after killing her husband she had sewn both his eyes and his mouth shut with thin, red thread.

I tried to tell my mother over cereal one morning, but she was never one to believe in ghosts, and looked at the estate as a steal with its good amount of acreage and low price. She laughed and said that if she did not leave the city, my father would have the same fate as Mr. Wilson. She must have seen the nervousness in my expression, and was quick to tell me to relax, that the house was perfect. She got up from me the table with her Styrofoam bowl. "Don't blame the house."

* * *

I awoke early to the sounds of what I assumed was my mother moving furniture below my room. I staggered down the stairs to see what she was doing. Partially due to my groggy state, I was startled to see that the den and all the rooms on the first floor had not been touched, but the noises continued. Looking to the right of the staircase, I saw the basement door was ajar. I swallowed a growing knot in my throat and walked towards it. The lights were off, but the noises only got louder. I called down for my mother, but there was no response. Trying not to let my fear get the best of me, I called down once more, "Mother, this isn't funny! What are you doing down there?" Still there was no answer, but the sounds paused, and I heard the floorboards beneath my bare feet creak.

Still hoping it was my mother playing a prank, I rolled my eyes, grabbed my coat from the rack by the front door, and exited the front door. Stepping out onto the porch, I yelped, feeling a stabbing sensation in the center of my foot. From the arch of my foot I removed a small needle threaded with red sting. Assuming this to be part of my mother's game, I tossed it into the overgrown shrubs beside the house. Instead of playing into her game, I took the opportunity to explore the grounds. Crossing my arms over my chest, I walked towards the pond in the backyard. It was not as large as it appeared in the pictures, and it was much dirtier than I had imagined. I sighed and stared into the murky water at my reflection. I assessed my bedhead and pushed a disobedient bang behind my ear. I took a step back as a tail of a fish broke through the surface, startling me and distorting my reflection. It wasn't until the tail was disappearing that I thought I saw a thin, red thread trailing behind it.

"Good morning, Annie!" I heard my mother call from across the pond. She was wearing yellow gardening gloves and pulling up weeds from behind some bushes on the edge of the property. "Come here and look what I have found!" I was thankful for the opportunity to get away from the pond and my fearful imagination.

When I reached my mother, she was bent over, brushing some fallen leaves away from a stone by her feet. "I found Mr. Wilson!" she shouted and laughed as she began reading the stone in a mocking tone. "Here lies Martin Howard Wilson, beloved husband and pillar of the community." She laughed again. "Well not too loved, considering she killed him."

"Stop joking about it, Mom." I fastened my arms tighter across my chest.

"Oh, relax Annie. She's dead. She can't hurt me." My mother rolled her eyes.

I looked over the bushes that separated me from my mother and glanced down at Mr. Wilson's grave. My mother continued to pull up the weeds around the headstone. Sensing my anxiousness, she snapped, "Quit your worrying, Annie."

I turned away from her to walk back to the house and away from her teasing, but quickly remembered the events from the morning. I turned around to face her. "Hey, were you moving things around in the basement this morning?"

She looked back at me, puzzled. "No, I've been out here since I got up. I went to meet the neighbors earlier. Why?"

"No reason." I do not know why I did not simply tell her the truth.

Seeming to ignore my question, "The neighbors said that Mrs. Wilson hung herself from one of the beams in the work-shop on the anniversary of her husband's death." She wiped some sweat from her brow. "I think we should go down there. You just need to beat your fear at its source." Feeling confident with that solution, she turned away from me and went back to tending Mr. Wilson's grave. She tossed a weed over the bushes, and I could have sworn I saw a red thread tied to one of the roots.

* * *

I woke midday again the next day to a silence that I had never experienced. I blamed this on living in the city my whole life with a mother who insisted on being active as soon as the sun was up. I sat in my bed for an extra moment, contemplating the cause of such a quiet morning. I assumed my mother must have been sleeping in, tired from all of her yardwork yesterday. I chose to believe this, even though in the back of my mind I heard my father complaining about how annoying it was having to share a bed with an early riser. I rose from my bed on a mission to wake my mother and start the day.

As I reached for my doorknob, I saw a red thread tied around it. I blinked repeatedly, assuming my imagination was playing tricks once more. When I reopened my eyes, the thread was still there. My mind immediately started thinking of logical explanations, and I remembered my mother's plan about beating my fear. I rolled my eyes and opened my door, only to find the string tied to my doorknob connected to the banister of the staircase. "You are so funny, Mother!" I shouted, as I descended the stairs.

At the base of the stairs, I found another thread bowed around the last railing, connecting to the door leading to the basement. The door was opened all the way, and the lights were on. This comforted me, and I laughed as I walked down the basement steps. "I get it, Mother. I need to stop being frightened by the—" My breath hitched in my chest as I saw my mother laid out on a table in the center of the room in the same clothes she was wearing yesterday. "What are you doing?"

As I continued down the stairs I noticed a red string zigzagging all over her body. I proceeded slowly to her side, letting my fear and curiosity get the best of me. "How did you—"

I stopped. Her body looked like a pin cushion. It had been stuck with too many needles to count, each one standing upright in her skin and threaded with red, creating the zigzag pattern. A chill seized me as I moved towards her head. Both her eyes and her mouth had been sewn shut.

WE ARE OUTNUMBERED BY THEIR DEAD
JULIANA GRAY

SOME OF THEM were hunted. Some were hit by cars. Some starved, hard as that is to believe, with does leaping garden fences, fawns grazing on campus greenspaces, tall bucks feasting on sunflower seeds tongued from bird feeders. And yet.

Once, a button buck wandered through the open back doors of the Science Center. His hooves clicked like a debutante's heels on the tiled floor. Then a secretary emerged from her office and the deer took off. His hooves slid and skittered as he ran, panicked. Hearing the racket, professors and students filled the hallway and tried to herd the animal back out the doors. They stood warily, hands extended, laughing—really, it was very funny—as the deer raced around and around until it took a bad corner and crashed into a table of Psychology handouts. The people stood back, waiting, but it didn't run again. Its thrashing heart had given out.

Once, a student found a baby fawn curled tight as a ball in the high grass behind his dorm. Thinking it had been abandoned by its mother, the student gathered the fawn, all spots

9

and spindly legs like downy chopsticks, into his arms and carried it into his building. He and his friends made a nest of towels in the common room and settled the fawn into it. They took pictures, Instagrammed, Facebooked, Snapchatted. They asked each other what they should do. Did fawns drink milk? Cows' milk? Should they call Dr. Cardinale from Bio? Dr. Beaudry from Environmental Studies? Could it be tamed for a pet? Meanwhile, the mother doe outside circled the dorm, sniffing the air, frantically searching. When there was nothing left in her mind but mad, buzzing frenzy, she leaped through the plate glass window, crashing into the common room. The students screamed. The doe staggered blindly, crimson gouts spattering the ugly furniture. Her foreleg was broken. One great wedge of glass jutted from her eye. She lunged and snorted and finally fell inches away from her fawn, which remained obediently motionless as its mother's lifeblood soaked the industrial carpet.

Do you believe this? Are you listening? We have heard them running through woods without snapping a twig. We have seen them sleeping in the long-dead grass of parking lots. We have seen them walk through the walls of newer buildings, passing through the kitchen of Ann's House, slipping away into the bricks of Miller Theatre as easily as Hamlet's father.

How many have died? How many remain? You can see them at daybreak, stepping delicately across icy sidewalks. You spot them, too late, beside the highway, their flanks quivering with indecision. Sometimes they leap. You slam the brakes, hear the solid thud of impact, but when you pull to the shoulder the deer have vanished, your fender is undamaged. The only sounds are your ticking engine and your own ragged breath.

Look for eyeshine. Those are alive. Look for plumes of breath in winter, scat in summer.

At night, you can see them in the fields, grazing on air, glowing blue with the cold light of extinguished stars.

TFW Bae is a Ghost

Juliana Gray

D EAR PROFESSOR,

I know I've missed a bunch of classes lately, and also probably some assignments like the paper that I think might have been due today. I don't want to make excuses, but I have been going through a lot of stuff lately. I got very bad food poisoning from Ade that caused me to miss several classes. Then I got a concussion from sitting up too fast when my roommate set off an air horn in the middle of the night and I hit my head on the shelf I put over my bed to hold my protein shake mixes. Also I do not think the university should have classes before 11 a.m. because it is too hard to wake up that early, but that is another issue. My main problem is my girlfriend.

You may not believe this, professor, but I'm going to be honest with you: I think my girlfriend is a ghost.

Now, I know what you're thinking, "Yeah sure, Jared, what have you been smoking?" But hear me out. Everybody knows Alfred University is haunted AF, but I never gave it much thought. You'd hear about somebody seeing a ghost in

13

the Brick or the Steinheim castle, but I figured those people were just tripping. Until it happened to me.

Back in the first or second week of the semester, my English class was doing one of those dumb "learn where the library keeps magazines or dinosaur bones or whatever" exercises, when I saw this fine female sitting at a table by herself. She looked like she was reading, but I was like, no way anybody has to read a book this early in the semester, so I went to talk to her.

I was all, "hey girl, what you doing?" and she was all, "reading this book," and I was like, "you'd look really pretty if you'd smile" and she was like, "please, I just want to read." You know, playing hard to get. But I could tell she was into it. She had long hair, kind of red or brown or blonde-ish, and looked like she had some serious curves under all those sweaters and scarves. She didn't say much, but I figured she was just being mysterious, like an art student.

I sat down on the arm of her chair and kept asking questions and trying to get her number, and just when I felt like I was getting somewhere, I heard this voice behind me. "Jared? Have you finished the resource scavenger hunt yet?" It was my professor, totally killing the moment. I got up to tell her I was almost done, I was just asking this library patron the way to Special Collections. Then, when I turned back around, the girl was gone. Just vanished!

The next time I saw her was at a lecture I was required to go to for my sociology class. I was sitting in the back with my boys, texting and looking at dank memes while this lady on the stage went on and on about feminism or something. Then I saw her, that fine girl, wearing that same big knot of scarves, sitting by herself and staring straight ahead.

"Watch this," I told my boys, and I eased out of our row and went to sit next to her. She just barely looked at me, playing it cool, but I could tell she recognized me. I tried talking to her, but she just sat silent, looking straight ahead and taking notes. It was like she couldn't even hear me.

This might be more information than you want, professor, but I gotta tell you, I was pretty thirsty. Plus, all my friends were watching, so I had to show them how it's done. "You're beautiful! Smile! Just give me your number!" I whispered to her, and passed her my phone. Finally she took it, and when her fingers brushed mine, they were cold, like Otter Pops.

When she handed the phone back, she'd put in her digits but not her name, so I saved the contact under LIBRARY SMASH. Then the lecture finally ended, and while I was signing the attendance sheet, she vanished again. Like, one second we're getting to know each other, the next second she's gone. That was the second time she'd disappeared like that. It was what you, professor, would call ironic.

And here's where it gets really creepy. I tried texting that number she gave me, but I got an error message that it was a land line. So I actually called, and it turned out to be the number for a funeral parlor.

A funeral parlor! Like, where dead people go! *Because she's a ghost.*

But I didn't get it yet. I figured she just gave me the wrong number by mistake, and now she was probably disappointed that I hadn't called her. So after that, I was low-key looking for that girl everywhere. I went to stuff on campus that I normally wouldn't be caught dead at because I thought she might be there. I went to an art gallery opening. I went to a Women's Studies Roundtable. I even went to a poetry reading. It was terrible, and none of it made sense, but I was determined to find that girl.

Then, finally, me and some of the guys were walking back from a party late one night, and I saw her. It was one of those foggy nights we get in spring, when the weather turns warm all of a sudden and the snow melts and the air fills up with clouds like a room full of people smoking weed. Which is exactly what I'd been doing, TBH, so she looked like she was floating over the sidewalk. Still, I just about lost it. "That's my girl!" I yelled to the fellas, and I took off running after her.

I remember how my feet pounded on that brick sidewalk, running past the King Alfred statue and up toward the castle. "Hey!" I called, but she didn't hear me. "Hey, girl! Slow down!" She just kept floating, so I ran faster, and finally I caught up with her.

I grabbed her arm, and she turned toward me really fast. Suddenly I felt this intense sensation. It was kind of painful and kind of amazing, like being kicked in the balls by a boot made of lightning.

The next thing I knew, I was lying on the ground with a splitting headache, and the girl was nowhere in sight. My friends had caught up and were trying to help me stand up. "Bro, you can't just sneak up on girls and grab them like that," one of them said. "She totally tased you."

But I know that's not what happened. I touched a ghost, and she accidentally hit me with some kind of supernatural energy. Like in *Ghostbusters*—the real one, not the girl remake.

Listen, professor, you're always going on about "critical thinking" and using "logical arguments" to support my claim, so that's what I'm trying to do here. It is a fact that I have never been rejected by a female who wasn't a stone-cold bitch.

Yet here is this girl who keeps disappearing when I try to get with her, whose phone number is a funeral home, and who zaps me with ghost lightning whenever I try to touch her. So as strange as it may sound, the most logical explanation is that this girl, who I am crazy in love with, is a ghost.

Or a lesbian. But probably a ghost.

So I hope you will excuse my missing work, and let me know when I can make up the exam. I don't know if Alfred has a ghost policy, like the one where you make A's if your roommate kills themselves, but considering how haunted this campus is, I think it definitely should.

Sincerely,
Your haunted & heartbroke student

A Ghost's Guide to Manners
Haley Ruffner

Section One: Dancing

As a young lady, you will be expected to attend balls, though you will find them few and small in Alfred. Mother's maids will string you up by your shoulder blades in a corset tight as a hangman's noose, paint your lips blood red, and send you in to waltz gracefully with men. The men will think you friendly when you lean on them, but you must not tell them your closeness is because your heels are much too wobbly to stand on your own. If your dancing partner becomes too forward, stumble so that your heel grinds into his foot, then look away, blush, and apologize for your clumsiness while he pretends not to limp on bruised toes.

The drink table will be frequented by older women whose dresses match the cups of wine they down while watching the young folks dance. They remember their dancing days before the apathetic husband and the children and the wrinkles around their eyes. I do not regret missing the chance to grow old and bitter. You will be expected to avoid the drinks and converse with the women, but you might enjoy the dance if you visit the drink table and avoid the women.

Section Two: Leisure Activities

Soon you will no longer be allowed in the garden to un-
earth bugs and worms with your little brothers. Mother
will dash them from your grip, send you for a bath, then fill
your hands with needle and thread and your head with su-
perficial gossip. You will be told that the garden is a place for
stately walks in pleasant weather during the few months it
does not snow. You will discover that the elbow-length gloves
your friends recommend for fashion hide dirty fingernails.

Mother will drag the old pianoforte to the center of
the parlor and hire a tutor to dance your marionette fingers
through country ballads and Mozart waltzes until you drum
your fingers through songs in your sleep. If you are not entirely tone deaf, you will be expected to sing along. Your mar-
riageability will decrease if you cannot carry a tune, but your
enjoyment of social gatherings will increase since you will not
be the sole source of entertainment. In some cases, it is pru-
dent to deny any musical ability.

You will be allowed access to the library and encouraged
to read. Father will warn you away from his advanced law
books, but if he catches you with one he will smile and leave
you be. When Mother plans social gatherings, be sure to stash
books throughout the house as a means of escaping unwant-
ed conversations later. Prepare to answer the question "What
are you reading?" with a polite, proper, and vague response.
No one will really listen unless you say something scandalous.
If Great-Aunt Millicent asks you four times in one evening
about your book, do not jest and say that you are studying
a prostitution manual. She may forget, but the rest of the
guests will not.

Riding will be allowed in pleasant weather and in the
company of friends. You must wear a riding habit and never
outpace the men in your group even if you have a faster horse

and better seat. Midnight gallops wearing men's pants and riding astride are absolutely prohibited. If you break a bone doing so, sacrifice your dignity and say you tripped on the staircase. Keep a schedule of the moon's cycles and go when the moon is bright. Designate a small sum for bribing the servants to take care of your horse in the dead of night and wash the riding pants.

SECTION THREE: DRESS

THE DAYS OF your loose nightgowns and unbound hair are over. Once you dressed for comfort, but now your clothing must reflect wealth and propriety as befits our family's status. Mother will tell you this, and you must nod and act pleased with the new dresses she orders for you. You may even like some of them. If you slice away their underskirts to lessen their weight, designate the washing thereafter to one maid you trust. (Theresa and Anna are trustworthy; Mary will sell you out to Mother.)

There is a jeweled hairpin I want you to have, in my bureau folded in with my red bonnet. Its ends are sharpened and will suffice if ever you need to defend yourself from prying hands.

SECTION FOUR: COURTING

REMEMBER THAT MEN will flatter you as a means to reach your dowry, not your heart. I am told that the green eyes Mother gave us are dazzling. You have Father's hair, raven-black, and though you envied my chestnut curls, I always wished I looked like you. You will be in full bloom by now, sister of mine, and you must know the difference between men who would water your roots and men who would cut your stem and leave you in a vase to admire your wilting beauty. Mother will approve of flashy men with wigs that shed powder when they walk and whose pockets jingle with coins. Father will watch you converse and approve of the men who most often make you smile.

Beware of older men who claim to be misunderstood or cheated out of a rightful inheritance. Do not make plans to run off with men named Gideon who claim to have a small fortune in the next county over. Men who must drink from a flask now and again to keep their hands from quivering are not, as they would have you think, recovering from a grievous illness. In most cases, such men will fumble at your corset and end the evening slumped unconscious in the shrubbery. When Father finds them in the morning, he will chase them off and you will never see them again. Our brothers will emulate their drunken stagger through the hedges for weeks thereafter.

You will meet men you like, men you dislike, and men you think you like. Be most cautious about men you are certain you like. If a man you dislike remarks on the pleasing swell of your breasts, compliment his breasts in turn, but do it quietly enough that Mother cannot hear you. When she asks what you did to offend him, say that you do not know. Later, when Father asks how you managed to run him off, tell him the story. He will roar with laughter from deep in his belly and clap you on the shoulder.

When you fall in love, follow every rule that Mother and Father set. Do not rush. Wear your hairpin always—however good his intentions are, he may need an occasional reminder that your tongue isn't the only sharp thing you have.

As far as midnight meeting-places go, avoid the gardens. Mother and Father's bedroom window lines up directly over the oak bench there, and even whispers carry enough to wake them. The stables are likewise impractical—the horses will carry on and wake a groom, who will give you a sound scolding.

I recommend the ballroom, but wear slippers to dampen the sounds of your footsteps.

SECTION FIVE: ON LOVE AND DYING

NEVER ARRANGE A rendezvous at the pond by moonlight with your fiancé. If you do, wear sturdy boots and do not stand at the edge of the pier where the boards are bowed and slick with dew. Do not wear the heavy brocade gown even if he has told you it's his favorite. Stand well away from the lake while you wait for him. Do not trust the brace poles on either side of the pier that you swung around and around as a child. They are worn now, rotted out beneath the water. You have always been more surefooted than me, less likely to take fright at things like a lover's whispered greeting, too practical to stand on the edge of a damp pier and balance against a decaying post.

I suspect you will avoid the place anyways, haunted as you will be at the sight of my pale bloated shell slumped at the shore. Its allure is untarnished for me. My name never sounded so beautiful as it did on his lips when he screamed it to the heavens, thrashing through the silt and cattails towards me. Silver-backed fish cradled me in my descent, nosing through the bubbles from my last breath. Dark brocade billowed up at first, buoyed by pockets of water, then bore down like a pair of crimson wings propelling me to the pond bed. He pulled me to the shore by the train of my dress while I watched from above. Make sure Mother and Father know that the fault is mine, the last and most reckless mistake I'll ever make. I slipped and fell, and my fiancé could not save me.

He will still be there when you arrive. Having called for help, he will cradle my body in his arms until you pry him away. Do not let him drown himself. He cannot follow me here.

I could not have chosen a more pleasant place to die. My lungs overflowed and shrieked, but the soft descent under the pale green algae moonlight felt like being rocked to sleep. So grow up, little sister, and fall in love, and stay away from this place until you are very old. I will watch and wait, and welcome you when your time comes.

PROWL
HALEY RUFFNER

L IEUTENANT KEVIN LOVELL lived on the fourth floor of the Brick, alone but for two aging goldfish drifting in a greasy tank. He was well acquainted with his neighbors through a complex schedule of eavesdropping and window-peeping. The young couple on one side, one art major and one biology, smoked so much marijuana he could sometimes get a little high if he lay on the floor with his nose pressed to the heating vent. Looking up from the sidewalk outside, he could see a glaze of smoke against their window, a choking fog curled on the pane like a sleeping cat. Their shower squeaked when it ran. They once brought home a dog that barked so incessantly he knocked on their door and threatened to shoot it, after which they got rid of it.

His other neighbor was an old nurse whose poor health and lack of noise made him sometimes wonder whether or not she was alive. Invariably, she would turn the radio on or flush the toilet and he would be relieved. Her alarm clock was set to its loudest setting—on infrequent mornings when it went off, he sat up so quickly in bed he saw stars. The throbs and cadences of her voice, in contrast, were so soft he had taken to keeping a stethoscope on the table next to their shared wall to listen. She addressed her visitors and patients as "honey" and "sweetheart" in a lilting accent that made him think of rocking chairs on a wraparound porch and sweet tea in sweating glasses. He wasn't sure if she was the type of lady who slept like the dead until her shift started, or if she rose at dawn to quietly pour herself some cereal and read the newspaper. He didn't like not knowing.

The thing that interested him most about his elderly neighbor, however, was a name he'd once heard her mention to one of the other nurses. "Amber, my granddaughter, comes to visit next week—she wants to see the campus before she decides on a college." The date of the girl's arrival shone in red ink on the calendar hanging in his kitchen by the goldfish bowl. He'd met Amber before, though he didn't know who she was then, and he lusted for another glimpse of the fiery-haired beauty.

His first encounter consisted of her brushing by him up the spiral staircase, light as sunshine as he trailed behind laden with ration bags. She wore a cotton skirt that clung to her legs and a draping maroon shirt he could see all the way through. Her hair hung in a silky braid the crimson of honeymoon sunsets. She talked much louder than her grandmother, but he used the stethoscope anyways, slumped against the wall panting after her voice like it was his own heartbeat through the ear pieces.

She was set to return today, and this time he was prepared. The floor was swept, the bedsheets washed, and the few intact bathroom tiles shone. He waited on the couch with glazed eyes, a coffee mug and open whiskey bottle arranged in a line on the polished coffee table. Seconds crept by until the girl was five minutes late, then ten. He tensed with every sound—the young couple next door pounded against squealing bedsprings, their frantic pace like running footsteps on the creaky stairwell. It was infuriating. He wanted to claw through the wall, but he had to wait and listen.

He smoothed down his combed and gelled hair, adjusted his collar, checked the new deadbolt on his door. A red knitted scarf of the old woman's sagged in his hands, pilfered from the laundry room weeks ago.

"Your grandmother gave me this and told me to tell you that she's not feeling well today. She's not up for company, but she asked me if I would take you to dinner instead," he'd say, presenting the neatly folded scarf to her. It would not be damp from his clammy hands, nor would it be creased with the evidence of his agitated grip on it. She would not question him. She would be taken in by his neat appearance and hospitality. She would come inside of her own volition, trusting a handsome, fit soldier in uniform. He would speak calmly, gently, so as not to frighten her nor let his voice carry through the wall to her grandmother.

When he made her scream, he would do it in the bedroom with the door bolted, and the couple on that side would only think he imitated them. When the building burned later that night, the firemen would say it was an accident. There would be no evidence of sweat- and gasoline-doused bedsheets. The flames' roar would drown out the howling as mortal flesh met eternity and balked from it.

Years later, a first-year student would tell her friends about a presence she felt in bed with her at night, but when she woke in the morning no one was there, her lock undisturbed. Her heartbeat would quicken when she felt him there, and though his stethoscope had burned with his body, he would latch on close enough to feel her thrill of fear or pleasure, her sharp inhales, the warmth of her soft body as she pulled the blankets closer. If she was not alone, he would shove himself between the bed and wall and ride the rock of the mattress, suspended in the heat of panting breath. He would stay with her until she fell asleep again, pressed up against her back, smoothing her eyelids closed with gentle bone-dry fingers.

PASS BY CATASTROPHE
NIC OSINOFF

C ARMEN TOLD ME she was going to kill Kathleen in Powell. She spoke as seriously as one could with a mouth full of mozzarella sticks.

I thought it was a joke. I chuckled, "Oh, jeez. What happened this time?" Carmen was always getting into spats with her roommate. Always over something trivial. Leaving dirty laundry on the floor, keeping the lights on past 10 p.m., eating each other's food, that sort of thing. They wouldn't speak to each other for a week over a disagreement on whether Meryl Streep was overrated.

Carmen took a swig of her soda and slowly scanned the room for witnesses. She then grabbed me by the shoulders and drew me in close. "I'm… failing macroeconomics." Her voice was gravelly, and I could see that her glasses were smudged and spotty.

I shook her hands off my shoulders with a laugh. "So, what? Is she not letting you study? Did she steal your books again? Just apologize for, like, blowing up the microwave or whatever and she'll probably forgive you and give 'em back."

29

Carmen shook her head while wagging a fry like a finger. I felt a splotch of ketchup hit my cheek. "No, no no no no. No. Listen. There's no way I'm passing macro. I'm screwed there. And that F's gonna destroy me, Layla. I'm already doing shit in Ethics. One more failed exam and I can kiss my scholarship money goodbye. Before I know it, I'll be starving on the streets, dude."

"Jesus, calm down, dude. What's your point?"

Carmen shoved the last mozzarella stick into her mouth and leaned in close. "Your roommate dies, you get an automatic 4.0."

"That's a myth, Carmen. It's just a thing in movies and—Jesus Christ, are you serious? Why am I debating this?"

"I'm serious as a fucking heart attack, Layla." She had a string of cheese caught in her braces.

Carmen was staring me dead in the eyes. Her eyebrows were so furrowed they nearly formed a unibrow. Good god, I thought. She's not fucking around.

Slowly I lowered my head into my hands.

"I know, I know," Carmen sighed. "But, listen."

I peeked between my fingers.

"No one's gonna miss Kat."

I closed my fingers up again. I screamed silently into my palms. What the hell. What the hell! "Carmen…" I put my hands back on my lap and sighed long and hard. "I know your morals are a bit, um, skewed, but there's a difference between breaking into Ade at night to steal all the hard boiled eggs and committing first-degree murder for an easy A."

Carmen clicked her tongue in disappointment. "So… I guess you don't want in, then."

"I, what?"

"Any witnesses get 4.0s too. I know Foundations has been giving you a rough time, Layla. You leave everything to me and you can rest easy. Maybe without the reoccurring nightmares about John Gill."

My heart pounded in my head. She wasn't wrong. I was doing pretty lousy in Foundations. But not, like, murder lousy. But Angie To's words rung in my ear: "Fail a course your second semester and you fail the year." I thought about the pen drawing I hadn't started yet. Good god, maybe I was doing murder lousy.

Kathleen was an art student, too, one grade above me. A total glassblowing savant, I don't think I ever saw her outside the studio.

Sure enough, she was there, all alone when I went down with Carmen on Thursday night. She had her hair tied back in a lazy bun and her eyes seemed transfixed on the flames before her. Like she could see the face of God in it. Maybe that's why I was crap at Foundations. I just didn't have my heart in it. Can't say I felt a connection to the heart of the universe while doodling a hot anime girl.

It was hard to really feel sorry for myself in that moment though. My mind was as numb as my body. The only sensation I felt was the tremor of my heart against my ribcage. I reached out as Carmen approached Kathleen, but it was more reflex than anything. I barely grazed the back of her shirt, and I kept my feet planted firmly where they were.

I didn't snap back to reality until Carmen grasped Kathleen by her bun. Every muscle in my body woke up. My mind flooded with primal screams. It felt like getting struck by lightning. I charged at Carmen like a bull at a matador, my arms outstretched, crying for Carmen to let go. Carmen gave me a look caught somewhere between utter shock and sick maternal pride as I pushed Kathleen headfirst into the gaping maw of the furnace. Her bun burst into flames and her face was caked in char. She didn't have time to scream before all the oxygen was ripped out of her lungs.

Killing someone's a lot easier than you'd think. Why people blow their funds on guns and knives is beyond me. I think the only real barrier's mental.

* * *

"The University has decided, as compensation for any psychological trauma experienced as a result of witnessing the, um, passing of Kathleen McKinley, to allot Carmen Silvera and Layla Wexler 4.0 GPAs for the current term, and relieve them of all currently owed academic payments."

Carmen hadn't told me about that last part. If she had, I might've been on board since day one. I cruised by in Foundations in the following weeks. Turned in my pen drawing half finished, and, just as Carmen predicted, the John Gill dreams finally disappeared. I just wish Kathleen would too.

It started in subtle ways. I'd catch reflections of her in the bathroom mirror, or the toilet bowl. I chalked it up to post-traumatic stress. I was getting three hours of sleep a night, max. My brain was not in any place it should have been, so of course I was seeing things.

As the year began to draw to a close, things actually began to pick up. Don't get me wrong, I was still seeing images of Kathleen's melting skull in my morning cereal, but with my academics out of the way, for the first time in my life I was free to focus on myself. I went to parties. I stayed up until dawn and slept till four in the afternoon. I started working out. I made friends with just about everybody. I was a brand-new Layla. I didn't speak to Carmen anymore, though. Every time I saw her, I'd feel myself shrink and revert back to my old self.

Worst of all, seeing Carmen made the visions of Kathleen flare up like a motherfucker. And I certainly didn't need that.

I spent the summer in therapy on my mom's insistence. I tried to assure her that I was fine, that I barely remembered the incident, but she wouldn't have it. I spent the sessions trying to avoid making direct eye contact with Kathleen's decomposing corpse in the corner. I made nice with the shrink, and I'd be lying if I said he didn't help. The visions were finally beginning to die down. No need for institutionalization. I'd be back to school in August.

* * *

August was unusually cold when I came back for my sophomore year. It served as a grim reminder, I suppose, that my days of hedonism were finally behind me. It was easier than I expected, honestly, getting back into the routine of actually doing schoolwork. Sure, my social life wasn't nearly as active, but I was beginning to remember why I chose to pursue an art degree in the first place. I think I was finally catching on to Kathleen's passion for her craft.

I had gotten back in the groove of things by break. I refreshed bannerweb every ten minutes, eagerly awaiting my mid-semester grades. I was waiting for my order at the deli when they finally popped up. It knocked the wind out of my chest. I scanned the list. A- in World Literature, nice, nice… oh! B in Print Studio? Wasn't expecting that, and in Glass…a D-. But how? If anything, that was the class I was working the hardest in. The instructors seemed to like me too. What was the deal? The world spun around me as I held back my tears. I jumped when the man at the counter called out my order. I scarfed down my sandwich as I walked back to my house, barely registering the taste underneath layers of rage and shame.

I had no excuses anymore. Harder became my home away from home. I would sleep in the glass studio if I could. Anything to improve my craft, finally make the instructors appreciate the effort I was putting toward my art career. It was difficult for me, glassblowing. Every time I would approach the furnace, feel the warmth of the flame dance across my skin, my arm hair would stand up in fear. It made me remember. I had to talk myself down from a few potential panic attacks. I hadn't seen Kathleen in months. I was getting better. I was getting better.

One night in November, I was working late on a ginger jar. It was a Saturday. I should've been out with my friends, but instead I was cramped up all alone in the studio, the leaping flames of the furnace as my only company. That was, until a voice out behind me.

"A-ha! I thought I'd find you down here."

My vision blurred as I recognized the source of the voice. My rod crashed to the ground as my hands went limp. Slowly, I stumbled around to look in its direction.

Carmen twisted a lock of hair around her finger as she spoke. "It's really nice to see you again, Layla. It's been ages, man."

"What do you want?" The words flew out of me before she finished speaking.

Carmen put her hands out. "Calm down, dude. I'm just here to chat. We ended things on pretty shitty terms."

"And by 'shitty terms,' you mean first-degree murder, right?"

Carmen sighed and perched herself on a bench. She pulled a gum packet out of her pocket and popped a piece in her mouth. She chewed loudly for what felt like ages, obnoxiously smacking her lips like a cow chewing cud.

I broke the silence first. "I asked you already, what do you want?"

"I'll be straight with you, Layla. Business school is still a bitch. And if I wanna—"

"You can't be serious."

"Hmm?"

"Again? Really? You wanna rope me into this again? Carmen, I was traumatized. I couldn't live with myself. I spent the whole summer with a shrink. I, I—" A familiar corpse rose from behind the bench. "I've been seeing ghosts."

Carmen stared blankly at me. "Christ, I had no idea. You seemed pretty excited about it beforehand. I mean, you're the one who—"

Kathleen's face contorted in agony. Her lopsided jaw spewed black pus as it opened in a silent scream.

"Stop! I know what I did. It was a mistake, Carmen. You got in my head and made me think what we were doing wasn't so bad, but it was. It was fucking murder, Carmen."

Carmen clicked her tongue and shook her head in shame. "That's too bad, Layla. I mean, my grades haven't been great, but at least I've got the excuse that business school is fucking difficult. You're worried about failing in an art class, dude. You spend all your time in this building creating finger puppets and making up languages to talk to birds, and you can't even get a good grade without killing someone. You need this more than I do."

I could see Kathleen grimace under the sea of maggots crawling out of her right eye. She looked straight at me with her left. I knew what she was thinking. Carmen was a narcissist, an emotionally abusive, cold-hearted killer, but worst of all, she was a pretentious twat. I thought back to my first year. She never had a single kind word to say about the arts. Always making fun of Kathleen for spending all her time at Harder, sarcastically chiding me for not getting a "real degree." Jesus Christ, why the hell were we friends?

I staggered a few steps toward Carmen. Kathleen reached out a boney arm toward me. She seemed to pull me forward against my will.

Carmen chuckled nervously. "Oh, sorry, man. Forgot you guys were always a bunch of oversensitive—"

The end of her sentence was muffled by a deafening crunch as the shelf behind her collapsed. Broken chunks of ceramic and glass littered the floor around me. I felt a piece lodge itself in my leg. I screamed. On top of the wreckage stood Kathleen. Normal Kathleen. No worms, no pulsating blisters, just a serene, satisfied smile stretched across her face.

We stood there in silence for hours, our eyes locked through the fog of dismay and unbridled joy. Tears cascaded down my cheeks and stuck in the creases of my smile.

I was finally free. Free from guilt. Free from Carmen.

Free from my glassblowing final.

THE KILN
NIC OSINOFF

WE FOUND THE kiln two Wednesdays ago. Sonya and I were helping Nate unload some pots when he starting yelling across the room for us. I was a bit peeved at first. Typical of Nate to run off and pull some stupid stunt while we did all the heavy lifting. When we finally caved and walked over, we found him standing in front of a rusted metal door with a shit-eating grin smeared across his face.

I'd never seen the door before, but then again, I didn't spend a lot of time in Harder. I looked to Sonya to get a better grip of the situation. She looked just as perplexed as I did. That was concerning. How'd she make it to her junior year without noticing this eyesore?

Before we could tell Nate off for distracting us from the work, his work, really, he had already turned the handle and thrust the door open. I saw the veins in his arm pop.

It was pitch black inside.

We watched as Nate sank into the abyss, completely disappearing before reaching out a hand to beckon us in. Sonya grabbed my wrist and the two of us followed him. It was a good twenty degrees colder than on the outside. I turned on my phone's flashlight and scanned the room. The walls were completely bare save for the loose chips of white paint that covered them like freckles. In fact, the entire room seemed empty, or so I thought.

Flashing my phone toward the far back of the room, I came face to face with my reflection on a massive industrial kiln.

"No fucking way!" Nate squealed in delight. "I've never seen one this big!" He ran up and threw his arms around it like a hyperactive child strangling the new kitten he got for Christmas.

I won't lie. Kilns, honestly, scare the fuck out of me. It's some sort of transgenerational trauma, probably from when my great grandfather got sent to Auschwitz. That's what I tell people anyway, and then they feel kind of bad for asking and drop the subject. You can bullshit your way out stuff like that when you're a psych major.

This kiln was no different. Worse, even. It looked like it hadn't been used in centuries. Rust coated its surface like an uneven tan. When Nate knocked on its mouth, it rumbled deep and loud. Sonya and I stood awkwardly by as he ogled it.

Sonya was the first to break the silence. "Uh, Nate? Do you, um, wanna be alone?"

I snickered.

Nate whipped around. He looked like he was surprised to see us there. "Oh, uh. Yeah. You guys, uh, go ahead. I'll be out in a bit."

Sonya shrugged. We filed out the room, gently closing the door behind us. Back to work, we guessed. Nate still had like six or seven more pots to unload. Each weighed six or seven tons.

When we were done tidying up the area, Sonya called out to Nate. No response. She took a few steps towards the door. "Nate! We're done! You owe us dinner! Come on!"

Still nothing.

"He's probably still getting his nuts off to the kiln," I suggested.

Sonya glared back at me. "First, gross, second, let's go get him. I'm fucking starving. Unpaid labor works up an appetite."

The door was heavy, heavier than it seemed when Nate had opened it. I called out into the darkness. My voice echoed back at me.

"Flash your phone at him. Let's hope he's still got his pants on."

I switched on my flashlight. Nate was nowhere to be seen. I looked back at Sonya, worried.

She stared back, visibly annoyed. "The bastard fucking ditched us. Typical. Used the damn kiln as a decoy to get us to do all his work for him. I bet he discovered the room ages ago."

I chuckled and shook my head, playing along with Sonya's typical pissiness. Behind me, I swear I heard a grumble.

* * *

I woke up the next morning at three in the afternoon. Shit. I missed Philosophy. I whipped out my phone and texted Nate, hoping he'd lend me his notes. I waited a minute. Then five. Then twenty.

I wrote to Sonya, "Hey, have you seen Nate today?"

"Don't you have class with him?"

"I missed it and he won't answer my texts."

"Huh, that's weird."

"Yeah, I know."

"Nate always writes back. Fast."

"YEAH. I KNOW THAT'S WHY I ASKED."

"It's the only thing he's good at."

"SONYA, JUST ANSWER MY QUESTION."

"No, JFC, I haven't seen him. Probably hiding out feeling guilty for ditching us last night."

I chewed at my bottom lip. She wasn't wrong. Nate was a flake, sure, but he was a flake who wrote back in a pinch. I pushed that to the back of my mind as I got dressed for my 4:20 class. He'd turn up sooner or later, I was sure.

Nate didn't show up to dinner. Sonya and I sat alone in Ade, chewing our pizza in silence. Neither of us realized how much he filled our conversations.

We decided to check on him the next day. Sonya banged rabidly on the front door of Tefft until a frazzled first year let us in. I decided I'd do the knocking when we got to his room. I knocked once. Twice. Three times. Nothing.

"Yeah, Nate's been out a while."

I turned around to see Aaron, Nate's next door neighbor. A short and scrawny guy I knew Sonya had a figure drawing class with. He was wearing a navy bathrobe and his hair was damp from the shower.

"When's the last time you saw him?" I asked.

Aaron clicked his tongue. "Probably the day before yesterday. I didn't see him, but he was on the phone and was like 'okay, I'm on my way' and I heard the door slam, so..."

"Yeah, that was me," Sonya piped in, "th—that he was on the phone with. You haven't seen him since?"

Aaron shook his head. "No, sorry. Listen, if he shows up, I'll let you know." He walked into his room and was about to close the door on us before he twirled around and caught it right before it slammed. "Oh, crap, I forgot. I think I saw his jacket in Harder this morning, the ugly one with all the cartoon penguins on it. So, he's probably still on campus, I'm guessing."

I glanced back at Sonya. Nate was wearing the jacket when we last saw him by the kiln. There was no good reason for him to leave without it. It was the middle of February, the highest temperature that week was still well below freezing.

We agreed to meet up at Harder after 5 p.m. When I got there, Sonya was already in the building. She was waiting for me down in the firing room, Nate's hideous penguin jacket in her hands. She twisted it back and forth like she was wringing out water. Her eyes seemed fixed on the middle distance.

"You think he's still somewhere in here?" I asked.

She didn't respond. I followed her line of sight and realized she was staring toward the hidden kiln room.

"You... think he's still somewhere in... there?"

She shrugged. "Worth a shot, right? It was the last place we saw him."

I couldn't really argue with that. As we approached the door, I felt the floor quake lightly below me. I stumbled a few steps before Sonya caught me. She looked as though she'd felt it too. I tried four times to pry the door open before Sonya charged at it like a human battering ram. As she crashed through the entryway, a pungent smell assaulted us. I plugged my nose and I felt my throat fill with bile.

Through my tears, I saw Sonya approach the kiln. I turned on my flashlight, took a deep breath, and followed her down.

The stench grew more violent as I walked. I had to stop in my tracks halfway because I couldn't breathe. I kept the light on Sonya. She was scouring every corner of the kiln for any sign of activity. It quickly became clear that this was futile. We exchanged a final, solemn glance before Sonya pried open the door of the kiln. The smell of decay was unbearable. I heard Sonya scream before retching her lunch onto the floor.

The inside of the kiln was just as empty as the rest of the room, but its walls seemed to pulsate, like some kind of organ. Sonya traced a quaking finger down the opposite side of the door. She drew her hand back in shock, bringing a long string of mucous with it.

From deep in the kiln I swear I saw something squirm. Only its silhouette, long and sinewy like a tapeworm, wide but thin. I screamed for Sonya to shut the door before bolting out of the building.

* * *

Sonya brought a sample of the mucous to the Chemistry Department to check out. It took them less than a minute to identify.

Water, epithelium, glycoproteins, amylase.

Saliva.

ALCOHOL VIOLATION
JULIE BARR

AUGUST 24, 2003

I KNOW IT'S ONLY the first day, but I already don't like my roommate, Ida. She creeps me out. I know I should give her more of a chance, but within the first three hours of us being in our dorm room together, she pulled out a bottle of Smirnoff and offered me some. Of course, I rejected. Drinking could end my college career before it even started. The impression Ida gives me is that her college plans only involve partying and having a good time. I hope she won't pose too much of a problem. I can always leave the room to get away from her, I guess. Thankfully, I met a girl named Alice during orientation. She came to my room so that we could go get dinner together at Ade and Ida would stop trying to get me to drink.

After having some questionable chicken, Alice and I decided to walk to each of our classrooms to familiarize ourselves more with the campus. As we wandered, I noticed that there were a lot of paintings in each of the buildings. There was a common theme among the paintings in both Powell and Harder. They were all creepy yet intriguing. I was drawn to one painting in particular. It showed an old president of

Alfred, and a small plaque identified the portrait as Boothe Colwell Davis. I know my eyes must have been playing tricks on me, but I felt like he was watching me. Alice came over and asked if I was alright. I was, of course. We continued walking around campus until we found each of our classes in Myers, Harder, the Science Center, and Herrick.

Man, there are a lot of stairs here. I stopped once I reached my floor to take a breath before heading towards my room. I saw something tucked away in a dark corner along the hall. Another old painting. I brushed the dust off, but there was no plaque on the bottom. As I walked towards my door, the painting stayed in my thoughts. Strange. I went to bed almost immediately. Last night, before I came to college, I had a pleasant dream for once. It was the first day of classes and there was a guy who caught my eye. He came over to my table in the library and asked me out. Then we went to the Jet and split a milkshake and had dinner together. The whole dream was very sweet, but not typical for me. Hey, I'll take what I can get.

AUGUST 25, 2003

ORIENTATION DAYS ARE very... interesting. They just want everybody to be friends and meet as many fellow students as possible. I guess I did get to see some people who I would enjoy being around for the next four years. But all I really want to do is look into some of the Alfred history that I heard a few people mention. Anyway, I did get to do some fun activities earlier today. One event was a combined obstacle course and puzzle. Alice and I found a few people that would join our team. Eric was one of these new friends. He had broad shoulders and disproportionally short legs which made for a strange physique. His attitude and laugh made it seem like whoever he talked to was the center of his world. He distracted me just enough that I would start to drift away. I'm still not sure if this is a skill or an issue.

I went to dinner pretty late, Alice came with me. As soon as we walked into Ade, Eric was standing there. He waved at us. We grabbed slices of pizza and sat with him. Some of Eric's friends showed up. I shouldn't even be thinking about anything starting with Eric, but I guess I can't be blamed for dreaming.

After dinner Alice walked back to Reimer with me, but even she didn't want to risk a run-in with Ida. Nobody could blame her—Ida hasn't shown up to any of the orientation games or mandatory events. She's creepy. Once I unlocked my door, I let out a sigh of relief. Ida wasn't there. I ran and flopped down onto my bed without a care in the world. Instead of going to sleep like I wanted to, I scrutinized the room to see exactly where I would be living for the rest of the year. I looked underneath the shelf above my bed. It sat at a slight angle that made it seem like anything I put on it would slide off and onto my head while I slept. Underneath the board were notes from the mid-90s. Most of the notes were stupid little messages about somebody being in love. I thought about adding something myself, but I'll save that for later in the year when I have more stories to tell.

Last night my dreams were slightly more unsettling than usual. Nothing that I couldn't handle, though. One dream started when I was walking from the Annex towards the green monster (that's what they call the staircase up one of the larger hills here). There is a small bridge over a creek, but the creek was dry. Still, I could hear the rhythmic sound of water dripping somewhere. As I crossed the bridge, it started to crumble beneath me. I was stranded in the middle on a small fragment that floating above the rocky ravine. Instead of panicking, I just sat down and looked up at the sky. I waited in that position until I woke up.

TODAY WAS THE first day of classes. Being an engineering major, I was anticipating that even the syllabi would be overwhelming. However, I was pleasantly surprised. I think I can manage my workload this semester. I'm only taking 16 credits, but for some reason my parents thought even that was too much.

I noticed that most people were distraught the last couple days from being on campus and away from their parents for the first time, but to me it was freeing. Whenever I was home, my parents always wanted me to watch my younger siblings, and if there was even a second that they didn't think I was doing exactly what they wanted, well, everything changed. The firm grip on what I did throughout the day changed to a firmer grip on me. It was never bad enough to leave any marks, and if there was even slight evidence of injury there would be an excuse—something about softball practice that could account for a bruise. It wasn't often that things would get that bad, but when they did I would take the brunt of the violence for my brothers and sisters any day of the week. So obviously after the first day of classes, I was not expecting a call or even a text from my parents checking up on me.

In each of my classes, I went in and tried to find somewhere I could sit and still see the board, but from a distance so I could go unnoticed by everybody. I thought that positioning myself like that would allow me to avoid contact with people.

I saw Eric again, but this time he wasn't distracted by anyone else. He was walking directly at me and even sat down and put his arm around me. I could only stare at him—we were just friends after all. Then I noticed that he was waving his hand in front of me and asking if I was still on planet Earth. That's when I realized that he was sitting across from me, and he made a remark about being surprised that we had a class together. He was a biology major, but this chemistry class overlapped. I guess I did look pretty out of it, because Eric said he just wanted to double check that I was doing alright. I was, of course.

The professor talked about what he expected from us as students. Then we left the room only to trudge into the next classroom for the same boring process. As soon as my classes were over, I went to Powell for lunch. I felt strangely relaxed sitting in a room full of people. Everybody was still trying to figure out their friend groups, so no one was super loud and obnoxious yet. I sat down and ate my lunch, reading over my different syllabi. I wasn't worried. Walking out of Powell, I saw that painting of good ol' Davis again. This time I was conscious of how much time I spent looking at the painting so that people didn't think I was a weirdo. I knew that's what Alice thought, even if she hadn't said so. But what could I have said? History is fascinating?

My plan for the rest of the night was to just relax and watch some funny television shows, but I was more exhausted that I thought. It was around 5 p.m. when I decided, after the next episode, I should get dinner. That's when the door slammed so hard that the frame shook. It was Ida coming back from who knows where, but this time with a bottle of Jack Daniels in her hand. I asked what was wrong in a hope that she wouldn't get a noise complaint filed on us, but she just turned and stared at me. At first I was focused on the bottle, but then I jolted back. Her eyes were smooth and dark like obsidian. It must have been the lighting, but as Ida shifted, she looked exactly like my mother. She dragged her feet across the floor still clutching the bottle. She lifted it with a robotic precision the closer she got to me. She swung the bottle right down over my head. I closed my eyes to prepare for the impact.

I opened my eyes then. I sat up from my bed, breathing heavily. It was 2:17 a.m. and Ida was sleeping peacefully across the room from me. Somehow it was all a dream, but did I really think that she was capable of murdering me? I hope not.

SEPTEMBER 14, 2003

AFTER A FEW weeks of classes, I started to understand why my parents didn't think I would be able to handle this. There were times I couldn't seem to focus, even when what I was doing should have been relatively simple. I just have to power through until I reach the first break. I have no intention of going back home, but I am looking forward to visiting Alice's hometown so that I can relax and not have to worry about anything for a few days.

The days felt so monotonous to me. I would wake up and have breakfast with Eric, then walk to chemistry with him. Generally, that was one of the most relaxing parts of my day. He was so genuine that our conversations just flowed. On one day we talked about different animals that we wished lived on campus so that we could pet them, but on another day I would find myself pouring some heavy details of my home life on him. He nonchalantly would mention that he is there for me if I ever needed anything. I have tried to tell myself that he isn't interested in me, that my brain is playing tricks on me, but sometimes I do wonder if something could happen between us.

Today, I went to Powell after my classes to eat more crunchy pizza, but everybody has their social groups now. I'm not part of any of them. So, I just kind of sat in silence with my book. I couldn't really complain about being alone. I did it to myself. It wasn't that bad after all. I still have Alice and Eric to give me some comfort. I wasn't really reading my book at that point—I was staring at the words while my head wrote its own stories. I decided that I could have been doing the exact same thing in my room, so I tucked my book into my disorganized backpack. My feet felt heavier than usual, so I tried to focus on what was around me instead. I gave a little nod to the painting of Davis and went to throw out my trash. Then something behind me caught my eye. It was the painting again, but this time I could have sworn it was moving out of the frame. I told myself it was just another one of the tricks my brain played, so I started towards the door.

Something tapped on my shoulder. I remembered that both Eric and Alice were only just getting out of their classes now, so I had no clue who it could be. My legs were off before my brain could even process what I was saw. Whatever tapped me carried some resemblance of my father. All I could hear was shouting. All I could see was his tightly clenched fists at his sides. I tried to get away, but no matter how fast I tried to run, he was there pulling me back towards him. I looked down and saw an arm gripped tightly around my wrist. I went crashing into the ground. Everything went black.

SEPTEMBER 15, 2003

WHEN I WOKE up, a crowd of people surrounded me, and someone was holding me up. My eyes shifted back into focus. Alice was crouched over my head, and Eric had his knee under my back and was supporting my head. I asked them how long I had been out. They said it was only a few minutes. The room of people swarmed around me like insects. I felt fine. There was no reason for everyone to be staring at me like this. I started to stand up, but it took me longer than I expected. As soon as I was completely up, two paramedics rushed towards me. They kept asking me if I was alright, or if anything hurt. Like always, I am fine. They wouldn't accept that simple of an answer, so they tested me, asked me questions. Just as I had suspected, everything was negative. They finally left me alone. I just wanted to be alone. It was silly for all of those people to be inconvenienced just because I was tired.

I rushed back to my room trying to avoid everyone including Alice and Eric. I told them both I just needed some rest and that this all happened because my blood sugar got too low and I didn't get enough sleep. It was only 2 p.m., but I just wanted to go to bed. I turned off the lights, locked the door, and tried to sleep. However, I just found myself staring blankly out of the window, watching as the trees swayed in the breeze. I drifted into sleep eventually and stayed there until my mother burst into the room. Why was she here? She had no consideration for anyone, especially me. I tried my best to stay out of her way, but she would hunt me down even at college. I rolled over and saw that she had a bottle of vodka in her hand. She walked towards me. I couldn't even understand what she was saying.

She'd never listen to me. No matter how much I avoided her or tried to do the right thing, she'd still take out her problems on me. I sprung up from my bed and grabbed the bottle from mother's hands. She fought back. It made sense her alcohol was worth more to her than I was. Her grip slipped slightly, and the bottle slid out of her hands. Without any hesitation I held the bottle up and let it fall on her head again and again. It broke, but I kept going.

Someone knocked on my door. It was Alice. She asked me if I was doing any better, and I told her I still wasn't feeling well. Upon hearing that, she let herself in. Mother must have unlocked the door. I told her mother had come on short notice. The expression on Alice's face was horrifying. She just stared at me, and I couldn't realize what was wrong until I looked down and realized it was Ida on the ground in a pool of blood.

THE BLACK KNIGHT
CATHERINE DONAHUE

I SAT IN MY room, waiting for this new roommate to show up. I hated the idea. I had been living alone since September. Why did I have to learn to get along with a complete stranger? Resident Life hadn't even given me much of a heads up; an email 24 hours prior to his arrival. Honestly, I wasn't too impressed with them at the moment.

The door knob started to jingle, and he walked in through the door. He looked up, saw me, and nodded. "Sup man? My name's Dylan," he mumbled.

"Hey, I'm Tyler—or Ty—whatever works really. Need help moving in?" I tried to be friendly.

"Nah, I don't have much. Just a few bags and a fridge."

"Alright. If yah need help, let me know. I don't have class for the rest of the night."

"Thanks."

I went back to playing games on my computer while Dylan slowly moved all his stuff into my room. He didn't have much, but I still didn't like the idea of having a new room-mate. This room had been my space for too long to just hand over half of it to this guy.

While Dylan was organizing his stuff, I took out my head-phones. "So, what's your major?" I asked tentatively.

"I haven't decided yet—just trying to figure stuff out."

"Oh, I'm an engineering major so you know—lots of work and stuff." I tried to make conversation with him. He nodded his head but didn't reply. I figured he was just focused on unpacking.

Later that night I was sick of the silence and I was curious, so I asked, "Why'd you move out of your old room?"

Dylan looked up from his laptop with a blank stare. He sat silent for a few seconds, thinking about the question.

"I guess me and my old roommate just didn't get along well enough to continue living together," he replied.

"Oh, that sucks. Well I hope we can get along, but I'm not gonna lie. I really liked living alone, but it'll be nice having another friend."

Our conversation ended with a very unenthusiastic "yeah" from him.

I was hoping this kid would become a new friend of mine, but the more I tried to have a conversation with him the less I thought that would come true. I guess he was just as bummed about moving rooms as I was about getting a new roommate. At least I was nice to him.

About a week after Dylan moved in, I woke up to my blankets and pillows completely off and thrown onto the floor between our beds. Confused, I sat up, looked at the clock, which read quarter past seven in the morning. I looked at Dylan's bed; he was still sleeping. It was a Saturday morning, so we were both trying to catch up on our missed sleep from the week. I've never done it before, but I must've just thrown everything off during the night. I got up, picked everything up and went back to sleep.

I woke up again, three hours later, to find that all of my blankets and pillow had again been thrown off of my bed and onto the floor. But this time when I woke up, Dylan had left. Just as confused as the last time, I picked everything up and decided to stay awake and start my day.

Life with Dylan isn't as bad as I thought it would be, aside from the weird shit he does almost every week. I almost never see him in the room, and we speak even less. I was sitting on my bed doing my homework one night, when I got up to go to the bathroom. I didn't take my keys with me, because I never lock the door if I'm staying in the building. When I came back, not even five minutes later, I found the door had been locked.

I was so annoyed. I pounded on the door waiting for Dylan to open and explain why he was an asshole and locked me out. After not answering for what felt like forever, I heard someone walk up behind me. "What are you doing?" It was Dylan.

"What do you mean what am I doing? What are you doing? Why would you lock the door while I was pissing?" I couldn't hide the anger and annoyance in my voice.

"What are you talking about? I didn't lock the door. I ran down to get a drink."

I looked down and saw the Sprite in his hand and didn't see keys in the other. "Well how is our room locked if neither of locked it or brought our keys?" I snapped.

"You tell me. You've lived here longer," he snapped back. He pushed past me and jingled the door. It opened on the first try. "You were saying it was locked?" Dylan asked, confused.

"It was." I pushed past him into the room and sat on my bed. I didn't know why the door wouldn't open. I didn't understand. I tried at least ten times, and it wasn't opening. Annoyed as hell, I put my earbuds in and continued watching Netflix.

It was stuff like that. Weird things just continued to happen in the room, but only in the room. Once I came back and all of my posters and pictures had been taken off of the wall. None of this stuff happened before Dylan moved in, so he had to be the one pulling the stupid pranks on me. I started to understand why his old roommate kicked him out if he was doing this shit with him too.

The final straw came the Thursday before winter break. I came back to my room, and it looked like a tornado had gone through it. My clothes were flung everywhere, my bed was messed up, my posters were ripped down again. Dylan's shit was everywhere too. I didn't understand what the hell went through that kid's head. Why did he feel the need to make a mess of not only his stuff, but mine? When my blood had just about come down from a boil, the door opened. Dylan walked in. I whipped around and saw the look on his face. He looked shocked, but also scared.

"What the fuck dude? Don't touch my shit. I thought that went without saying." I practically screamed.

"I…This…It…" He couldn't seem to get any actual sentences out.

"I don't even care. Just pick up your shit and don't touch mine again. If you do, I'll be living by myself." I was beyond pissed, but he looked concerned, so I let it go for the most part. I was going to be away from this freak at the end of the day tomorrow for an entire month and it couldn't come soon enough.

* * *

I dreaded coming back after break because I would have to spend the next semester living with Dylan. I keyed into our room, half expecting him to be sitting there or something, but he wasn't. I looked around. Only my stuff had remained in the room. Confused, I looked around some more. I noticed an envelope sitting on his bed with my name scribbled on the front. Hesitantly, I picked it up and turned it over. Someone had written For Tyler's eyes only." Sealed and taped shut, this envelope haunted me. What could be in there? I mean, this kid was weird. Finally, I got the nerve to open it:

Tyler,

I know you must be confused. I moved out after winter break and back home. I didn't know what I was doing at Alfred University, except playing football, so I knew I needed to leave instead of wasting money that my parents don't have. I know the weeks I lived with you were strange, so I wanted to explain them the best I could.

Let me start with the confession that I was not the one doing all the strange things, but I think I know what was. At the beginning of the season, the upperclassmen football players convinced me to steal that Black Knight statue. You know, the one that was in Powell that went missing? Yeah, I stole it. I didn't know what to do with it, so I stuffed it in a bag and kept it under my bed. Soon, weird stuff, like what happened in our room, started to happen to me and my old roommate. We both thought the other one was pulling pranks and we ended up fighting over it which ultimately ended in me moving out. I was confused but didn't really care that much. When I moved in with you, I brought that statue with me because I didn't want to leave it with him. I should have.

When the same things started happening in our room, I was even more confused. I refused to believe that statue was haunted, but I started doing some research and it turns out it actually might be. I think that stupid statue is the reason everything weird started happening.

I couldn't bear to bring it with me, off campus, and back to my family because I love my family. I don't need anything happening to them. So, I left it with you. I don't know what you should do with it. Maybe try and return it or destroy it? I don't know. I just know these past months at Alfred have been awful for me because of that thing.

Anyways, good luck, man.

He didn't sign the letter. Maybe he just didn't want me to be able to blame the theft on him because I'm pretty sure that a signed letter can be considered an admission of guilt. He also didn't tell me where he left the statue which I also thought was odd. I began to look for it. I searched everywhere I could think of, until I finally looked in the cubby above his closet and found it hidden in the back corner. It was almost impossible to spot because of the dark steel.

I reached back and grabbed it only to be shocked by the coolness of it. I pulled it out and began examining it carefully. It was so strange looking. It was clearly broken in multiple places, missing both arms, one leg, and what appeared to be part of his helmet. Honestly, this was the strangest looking statute I had ever seen, and holding it was giving me the creeps. I don't blame Dylan for thinking it was haunted or for leaving it behind. But I didn't know what to do with it. I sat it on my desk, facing away from me, and went to bed. I would figure out what to do with it in the morning once I got some sleep.

I woke up and rolled over to find that statue staring at me. I jumped awake and sat there blinking, shocked. I know I had clearly faced it away from me last night, but I don't know, maybe I moved it in my sleep. I panicked slightly, then relaxed remembering spring semester classes didn't start until Tuesday.

I sat there staring at the statue wondering what the hell I was supposed to do. If I turned it in, I would either have to admit to stealing it or tattle on Dylan, but I doubt they would believe me if I did that anyways. I figured I would do some research on it, or at least try to. I pulled out my laptop and began searching Google. I couldn't find much on it other than some pictures of the statue with past students. It wasn't nearly as creepy then as it was now, since it had all of its limbs attached. I couldn't find any information on where it came from or why people thought it was haunted.

I soon became sidetracked and ended up watching Netflix until the sun was about to set. As I was getting ready to close my laptop, my stomach grumbled. I remembered none of the dining halls were open yet, so I decided to drive to Hornell and grab some snacks for my dorm room. Just as I was about to walk out the door, I had an idea. What if I brought the statue with me and threw it out on campus or on the road? That way someone would just find it and it wouldn't be my problem anymore. I grabbed the statue, threw it in a garbage bag, and heading to my car. I tossed it in my passenger seat and started the drive to Wegmans. I decided to wait until my drive back because it would be darker then and less likely that someone would see my throwing a bag out of my car.

I had turned right at the yellow blinking lights and was driving back towards campus.

* * *

Suddenly I awoke to find myself in what looked like a hospital room. My head hurt, but then again it felt like most of me hurt. I looked around and saw that I was surrounded by machines. A nurse walked in. "Oh, good. You're awake. I'll get the doctor," she said softly.

Shortly after, a tall man with a thick dark beard walked in and introduced himself to me. "Hi Tyler, I am Dr. Ross. Do you know where you are?" He looked at me with his large brown eyes.

"I mean, it looks like I'm in a hospital. But I don't know why." I had slight panic in my voice.

"Well, there was an accident. You appeared to have swerved off the road and run your car into a tree. You were pretty banged up, and we had to perform emergency surgery on your right leg. We were afraid you were going to decide to stay in that coma, but here you are, awake." He gestured to the bed. "Do you remember what happened?"

I moved the blanket off to find a fresh cast covering most of my right leg. "Not a clue. The last thing I remember I was driving back from Wegmans. What day it is? Are my parents here?"

"They are staying at hotel. We notified them and they will be in shortly. What day do you think it is?"

"Well the last day I remember it being is Monday. When I am assuming I wrecked my car?"

"Yes, you did get into the accident on Monday, but that was about a week ago. It's Thursday. Do you have any other questions?"

Of course I had questions. I had a million questions, but I didn't know which to ask first. "What caused the crash? Was anyone else involved?" I asked him hesitantly.

"No one else was involved. The police said it didn't really seem like anyone else was even on the road. It seemed you lost control of the car, drove off the road, and hit a tree. The people who lived up the street heard the crash and called 9-1-1. Shortly after the paramedics pulled you from the car, it went up in flames. Your parents have everything they were able to recover."

Just then, my mom and dad walked in. My mother ran over and hugged me, tears streaming down her face. I can only imagine how terrified she must have been.

"I'll check back in a little while." The doctor and nurse then excused themselves and went into the hallway.

My mom and dad sat and talked with me for a while, about a lot of things, including my car. I finally worked the nerve up to ask my mom, "So, the car is totaled huh? What were they able to save from it?"

"Well, the entire thing was burned by the time the firetrucks got there, but nearby they did find this statue. I think it's like a knight or soldier. Was that yours?" She looked confused.

My reply was almost too quick. "No. I have no idea about anything like that. I was just on my way back from buying some snacks."

PARALLEL TO THE PAST
TORI PELLEGRINO

I T WASN'T MY first time renovating a historical building, but it was my first high profile project since graduating three years ago. A grant from New York State gave Alfred University an opportunity to hire me to restore what they call South Hall. From what I understood, South Hall had served various uses over the decades. The records told me the building had been everything from a school house to a women's gym.

I accepted the renovation project without seeing Alfred's campus or South Hall itself. But such a high-profile contract would expand my portfolio tremendously and help put me in the running for more lucrative jobs, so I couldn't turn it down.

When I arrived on campus, I was in awe of how full the trees looked. The pines in the quad gave the perfect amount of shade for anyone seeking refuge from the spring sun. There were a few people milling around campus, no one was in a hurry to get to their 8:00 a.m. classes. Only a few professors and dog walkers were really up and about.

I was excited to see century-old buildings in such pristine condition. I appreciated the pride the university took in its history. I was, however, disappointed by the condition of

South Hall. The renovation proposal emphasized it was going to be an intense project, but I was still unable to hide my displeasure at such a dilapidated building. After assessing the structure and acquainting myself with the village, I settled in for the night at the Saxon Inn. I considered taking time to look up some history on the town, specifically the university, but was too tired from traveling and decided to get a restful sleep in my cozy hotel room.

Stopping by Physical Plant in the morning, I retrieved the keys to South Hall. As I expected, the inside walls were covered in graffiti. Some pieces were carefully planned, painted works of art really, while others were just spray painted profanities. The floor was littered with cigarette butts and trash left from kids with the munchies, but underneath all the dust and grime there was a building full of character. It seemed to be almost frozen in time with desks and chairs strewn about.

Almost every floorboard creaked as I made my way to the addition that was at one point the women's gym. This portion was to be torn down, but the rest was for me to return to its original glory. Sunlight peaked through the boards on the windows, illuminating the dust particles I stirred up with every step and giving the inside of the building a warm, welcoming glow. I stood for a moment to examine the beauty of the building. Inhaling the damp scent of rotting wood, I walked over to examine the floor of the recreation center to see if any of the original hardwood could be repurposed.

I stepped and heard an echo. I stomped again on the spot and was met with the same noise. I crouched down and peered into the spaces between the wooden floorboards. Using a spare piece of wood that had probably fallen from the ceiling supports, I was able to pry up the loose boards, causing a cloud of dust. Once my coughing stopped, I peered into the opening.

It revealed a rectangular trough with dirt walls and a dirt floor that had a solitary occupant; a statue of what appeared to be of a man, a knight, who seemed to be missing some features including an arm, a leg, and most facial details.

I pulled the object out of the floor and was blowing some of the dust off his armor to get a closer look when I heard screams and shouting from outside. Against the common sense of avoiding a potentially dangerous situation, I made my way back to the front door, wary of any other floorboards with secrets. Before I had even made my way outside, I could smell smoke. Not cigarette smoke, but the smell of a fire. I stepped out into a gray cloud and made my way down Park Street, but none of the students loitering around Herrick or Kruson seemed to be phased. I had not been in Alfred that long, but there was no way I could believe this was a normal day-to-day occurrence.

Coughing with each step, I made my way toward the source of the smoke. I stopped a student leaving the library to ask what all of the smoke was about. He simply replied that many people on campus vape, but there are no designated smoking areas, so the smoke tended to be all over the place. This much smoke seemed excessive to be coming from a few students.

I discovered the source of the screaming. Kanakadecka? Kanakadeda? Kanakawhatever Hall was up in flames. Yet, no one seemed to be alarmed. Students just walked past the building without batting an eye. They weren't even coughing from the smoke. As I approached, I pulled my shirt over my nose in an attempt to keep some of it out of my airways. Through the smoke, I could see a fire truck, but not the typical red or yellow ones. This one had wagon wheels, and a horse? I know this is a small town, but they must be more modern than that!

A few people stood by watching the commotion. A young woman was coughing while a fireman stood next to her, patting her on the back. All the people who were watching were dressed in white clothes, the women in dresses, the men in slacks and button-down shirts. It was an intense contrast to the denim jeans and purple and gold sweatshirts I had seen earlier in the day. As a group of young women walked by, I called out to ask why there was not more commotion about the fire. Some gave me a look of confusion and others a look of pity.

Ignoring their looks, I turned my attention back to the flaming building. Feeling the heat radiating onto my skin, I noticed a small face in the second story window. A young girl was trapped inside. I rushed toward the base of the building, hollering to the firefighters that someone was inside and needed to be rescued. No one seemed to hear me. I even tried shaking the firefighters, tapping on their helmets, screaming in their ears, but no one was responsive.

I decided I had no choice. Someone needed to help, and adrenaline gave me enough courage to storm the building. Feeling the heat through my clothes, I ran up the stairs into the second-floor classroom and was met with an entire class worth of eyes staring at me. I asked how they all could just sit and relax during a fire. The professor stopped her lecture to slowly approach me. She held her hands out and spoke softly as if trying to calm me down. How could anyone be calm during a fire, especially when one of this magnitude? The instructor laid her hand lightly on my shoulder, asking me if I was feeling all right. I faced her and screamed. Her outfit had changed from back dress slacks and a pink blouse to a long white dress with voluptuous shoulder accents and long sleeves. The panic caused by the sudden change in fashion momentarily distracted me from the inferno slowly engulfing the building.

The young girl was still gazing out the window. Looking past her, through the glass, I saw a sky blackened by smoke and ash. I called out to her, her serenity and calmness distracting me from the confused gazes of the students and concerned grip of the professor. The girl turned to look at me. As I escaped the sweaty clutches of the instructor and ran over to her, I could hear the wooden beams in the ceiling beginning to fracture. The building was going to collapse any minute.

I begged the girl to come with me to safety. She turned towards the window once again and spoke in a volume slightly above a whisper. I could barely hear her over my own coughing and the crackling of the flames. "Congratulations on finding the Black Knight. Now that it has been recovered, it can be displayed on campus where it belongs. It can continue to represent the campus community."

As soon as the final word had passed her lips, one final crack sounded and the building collapsed over me, the girl, and the entire class including the professor. Everything was black. I couldn't breathe. The pressure on my chest was unbearable, and I could hear my ribs cracking. I had made the grave mistake of letting all the air out of my lungs when I exhaled and was now unable to refill them with the oxygen I so desperately needed. Not that the air around me was worth breathing in. Though the darkness prevented me from seeing, I could still feel the dust and ash that was floating about settle into my face and get caught in my eyelashes. I needed to cough, but could not inhale enough to make it happen.

Implementing an old relaxation trick I occasionally used before a big meeting, I began to contract and relax each of the muscles in my body individually. Some extremities I could still feel and move while others I could not. I continued to lay there in the void of dust and black. With no air in my lungs,

I could not call out for the girl or the students in the rubble. My eyes soon began to play tricks on me. I was able to make out the outline of dancing flames taunting me and laughing at me for what had happened. Time stood still in that darkness. I was beginning to believe that I had died.

Then I heard the scraping of wood above me followed by the muffles sounds of yelling voices. Light emerged piece by piece as the wood above me was removed. I flinched slightly at the heat of the sun's rays, suddenly feeling like I was once again surrounded by fire. Slowly, my torso was unveiled, allowing room for my chest to expand. Unfortunately, I found myself still unable to do so and became panicked, the limited oxygen making me anxious. The rim of the wood that lined the pit I was resting in was decorated with people in various types of uniforms, all of them working to free my arms and legs. With the weight of the wood slowly being removed from my body, I was beginning to feel the extent of my other injuries. I could feel the tell-tale annoying sting of splinters and cuts. I had no clue what a broken bone felt like, but I could only imagine it was the shooting pains running up my legs. Two men pulled me out of my resting place, asking me if I was okay, if I could hear them. I thanked them for putting out the fire and asked if the young girl and rest of the class were okay.

"Miss, you were the only person permitted to be in the building at this time. We found no one else in our search," one man said.

Then another chimed in and informed me that the building came down, not because of a fire, but because the old roof finally caved in. I wanted to question and protest this information, but a woman in pastel blue scrubs placed a clear mask over my mouth and nose and instructed me to breathe as slowly and calmly as I could manage. The other paramedics stabilized my neck and removed me from the debris on a gurney. Once my eyes adjusted to the light, I could tell I was where the gymnasium that connected to South Hall once was, not Kanakapeda.

"Sir? Sir! How did I get all the way over here? I was in Kanakadela when it collapsed." My voice was muffled, and I doubt anyone could understand me. Then I remembered what the girl had said. "Where is the Black Knight? The statue I found? I need to return it to the university so the spirits can rest." I struggled against the restraints which held me to the gurney as they loaded me in the ambulance. "It's in the hole! It's in the hole!"

The firefighters whispered about the head injury I must have sustained during the building's collapse. Anything else they said was drowned out by the sound of the ambulance sirens as I was hauled off to the hospital. I was able to see the sky out of the windows on the back doors of the vehicle. There was nothing but blue skies for miles.

My time at the hospital passed slowly. I went through many tests so the doctors could assess the extent of my head injury. The neurologists tried to debunk my story about the statue. Every time I brought it up, they explained to me how improbable my story was. That the past and present could not exist at the same time. I finally gave in and agreed with the doctors that what I saw was just a result of hitting my head, so they would finally discharge me and permit me to return to work. Physical therapy would still be needed for my legs, but I was willing to say anything to be released. But I know what I saw. I didn't imagine those voices and that heat or finding the statue.

Over the next couple weeks the construction crew removed the debris from the collapse so a new renovator could take over the project. It took about eight weeks for a majority of my injuries to heal, though my legs were still in braces. I returned to work and my boss told me to take some time off after I raved on and on about the statue that was never found.

* * *

There was a newspaper on my desk, not the local one but The Alfred Sun. The entire front page was dedicated to an article about how the when the demolition of the gym addition of South Hall was completed, a secret compartment was found under the floor, and inside it was the infamous missing Black Knight statue with its missing limbs, completely undisturbed and covered in dust.

ERR

Anna Wiegman

"I DON'T UNDERSTAND why you want to go back to school so early. Don't you want to spend more time with all of us? It feels like you were only home for Christmas Day. You know how much I miss having you around."

"Come on Mom, I just want to have time to get settled and shovel my place out before classes start."

"You don't need a week to shovel."

"I heard that. You didn't even bother to say it under your breath."

"You know it's just 'cause I'll miss you."

* * *

Carlen O'Donnell sighed as she walked past her couch and flopped onto her bed. What a relief to be back in her apartment for the last week of winter break. It wasn't a big place, just an attic studio apartment with a bathroom, but it was cozy and quiet and, most importantly, hers. This apartment was her sanctuary. She loved her family—she really did—she just loved having her own space more. Getting back to school before classes started gave her time to rest; no worries about disturbed sleep or being tired before the semester even began.

As Carlen unpacked all the stuff she had brought back with her, she boiled water for instant ramen. Curling up with her hot soup in front of the small gas fireplace, she made a resolution to go shopping for real food tomorrow.

She loved the fireplace. Not only because it kept the apartment warmer, but watching the flames helped her to relax, even though it required sitting on the floor because of the pitch of the roof. She lay down after she finished her soup, not yet ready to go to bed and stop watching the fire.

* * *

She hadn't meant to sleep, but she woke the next morning in front of her fireplace feeling groggy with a massive headache coming on. Holding her head, she slowly got up from the floor. Carlen figured it was probably just a dehydration headache, nothing to worry about, as she poured herself a glass of water. The pain persisted as she made her grocery list, despite the water she was drinking.

"No, sweetie, none of us are sick here."

"I don't know what to do then, Mom. I have never had a headache this bad before."

"You should take some Tylenol—or you could always just come back home."

"Ha, drive there with this headache? I think not. I'll just see what I can find around here."

"Ah, well. If you are going to stop me from taking care of you at least go to the store and pick up something. I hate knowing you are in pain."

"Okay, Mom."

* * *

Carlen sat in the car with her head on the steering wheel debating if it really was a good idea to try to make it all the way to the store. She finally decided that her headache wasn't that bad, and she should be fine to do her grocery shopping. If she was getting sick, she knew she wouldn't want to go out for food, and it would be nice to be able to stay in until some of her friends showed up.

She trudged slowly through the aisles of the store, taking the time to get everything on her list including Tylenol. The lights overhead buzzed, and her headache seemed to lessen as she shopped. Maybe getting out of the house was what she needed.

Carlen only felt twinges now, but she kept her eyes hooded with her hand on the drive home. She struggled as she brought her groceries up the stairs all at once, and her hands shook lifting the bags onto the kitchen counter. Realizing her energy was fading, Carlen sorted her groceries into piles: "important to put away now" and "can be put away later." She tackled the former pile as she began cooking her dinner. Carlen's head started throbbing as she put some rice on the stove—maybe she had outdone herself today. When it was done, she scooped the rice into a bowl, steam swirling up as the surface was disturbed. She set the rice down as her eyelids drooped.

The fire winked at her out of its hearth; had she turned it on? She must have and just forgotten. It was mesmerizing, the way it danced. Flowing from one form into the next, the orange glow welcomed Carlen to come sit on the floor and leave her dinner forgotten on the table. She could almost hear the crackle of wood being eaten by flames, despite it being a gas fireplace. She curled up on the floor watching the flames waltz, drawing her in. Carlen's headache screamed for her to just go to bed—but she sat still, watching the flame. She wouldn't let any sickness take this pleasure away from her.

* * *

A spear of sunlight woke her up. She was on the floor. Her headache pounded. Why was she on the floor? Ah yes, fire. Carlen got up slowly. She should probably turn the fire off.

"Faithful servant, deadly master, does a fire make."

Carleen spun around. She hadn't said that—had she? No, she didn't think so. It wasn't her voice anyway. The room swam. She looked around to make sure she was alone. Yes, she was. No one else was there. Maybe she had said that, and just not realized? No, that couldn't be. Where could the voice have come from then? Maybe she was just lonely and imagined it. Yeah, that made more sense. Just a few more days and her friends would be back.

In the meantime, she needed to get over whatever sickness she had. She could make a breakfast of a nice simple bowl of canned soup and just take care of herself and shrug that whole instance off. Everything would be fine. Carlen wrapped her hands around her bowl of soup. She closed her eyes and breathed in the steam. Maybe she was getting a sinus infection. It didn't hurt like any sinus infection she had ever had before. Well, no matter what her headache was from, eating would help.

The rhythmic pounding in her head intensified with every sip. Carlen took some Tylenol, hoping it would give her a little peace. She turned towards the fire that she still had neglected to turn off. It crouched low in the hearth, reminding her of a cat getting ready to pounce. Now she was projecting life onto a fire. Maybe she should take a nap; the past two nights she had not slept well, falling asleep on the floor with her head pounding. Carlen crawled into bed, snuggling down under the covers.

* * *

She woke with a start, and then turned rigid—someone was watching her. Carefully she looked around, moving only her eyes so as not to alert the intruder. No one was there. Slowly she turned her head to see more of the room. Her apartment was empty. Her breath stuttered. Her heart lurched. What was happening to her? Tingles ran up and down her spine as she felt the unseen eyes rake over her. Someone was definitely in here with her. Or was it something?

On the verge of panic, she pushed her back up against the wall, pulling the blankets up to her eyes in a vain attempt to protect herself from the unknown. Hyperventilating, her head throbbed as her knuckles turned white, grabbing at her blankets to calm herself. Should she go home? No, she didn't want to go back to her family—her mother would have too much to say about that. She couldn't really stay here though, could she? Not with the something now in her apartment with her.

And yet. What if Carlen could show whatever this something was that she, Carlen, was the boss? That this was her apartment, and she wouldn't be scared away? Yeah, she needed to prove herself and push the presence out and into a new place. She needed to live and be normal; be happy. Easier said than done, when she felt so sick, and so sure that the presence was watching her. Her eyelids flickered, and though she didn't really want to sleep, she found herself drifting off. Sleep took her.

Her dreams were disturbed by beeping—no, chirping—coming from far off. She woke up slowly, dreams slipping off her mind in layers. The chirp came again from much closer this time; it was high pitched and jarring. Was she being tortured by something? She didn't feel the presence as acutely as before, but there was a weight in her chest like something was sitting on her. Carleen started to cry as the beep came again. Her head hurt. Her eyes drooped. She just wanted to sleep.

Sobbing made her head hurt even more. *Chirp*. Letting out one last sob, she decided to get up and eat. There was a bowl of food already out on the table; a cold bowl of rice. Had she done that? No, she wouldn't have just left rice out. How did that bowl get onto the table? Eyes raked over her again and she had her answer. But why would whatever was watching her need to get out rice? She threw it out.

"Carlen."

She whipped around, stumbling from the pain in her head. Nothing was there. She definitely heard something, but nothing was there. Carlen was being tortured, feeling a hand close around her chest. Don't panic. Stay. Not trusting any of her food anymore—the something could have tampered with all of it if it was able to get itself a bowl of rice—Carlen threw all her food out. The something couldn't poison her if she didn't eat. She would win.

Sitting down on the floor with her back against a wall, Carlen watched the fire. She was safe as long as she had her fire on. The flames jumped for her, emitting a warmth that made her forget her panic, though her chest still felt confined. The fire became the only light in the room when the sun had gone down. The weight on her chest worsened, chirping constantly interrupted her thoughts. The something, it wanted her out of here. She wouldn't let it have the satisfaction. This was her space. This place would stay hers. No amount of chirping or watching would deter her. Still, the hand squeezed at her lungs.

The chirping kept changing where it was coming from, the room shifted around her, but the fire remained her tether— *Chirp*—its dance lulling, calming, safe. Her head bobbed. She had to stay awake, to prove to the presence that she wasn't going anywhere. It would have to be the one to leave. Her eyes closed. *Chirp*. She shook herself. The fire leapt, dancing faster than before as it swirled towards Carlen behind the glass. The hand passed through her ribs, crushing her lungs and heart. Something would happen soon. The fire, it would come save her. She would not be the one to lose. *Chirp*.

* * *

"Hey, Mira, have you seen Carlen lately?"

"No, I was just going to go check on her 'cause I called but she didn't answer."

"Okay, tell me how it goes would yah?"

"Yeah of course."

Mira walked towards Carlen's apartment building. Mira knocked. There was no answer. "Carlen? Hey it's me, Mira. You weren't answering my calls, so I wanted to come check on you." *Chirp*. Mira stood by the door listening closely. What had that sound been? *Chirp*. There it was again. What could it be?

Mira tested the doorknob—it turned. "Your door is open Carlen, so I am coming in." She slowly opened the door and walked into the apartment. Something was very wrong. The air felt stagnant. It was too quiet. She screamed when she saw Carleen, red all over, still staring at the fire. Chirp. Mira looked towards the sound: The carbon monoxide detector LED flashed, spelling out ERR. It was chirping its end of life warning.

THE ROOMMATE
DANIEL FLETCHER

I MADE MY WAY to the Wellness Center, stopping short at the steps leading up to the door. I looked over my shoulder towards the Brick.

"No, I won't go back. Someone needs to listen to me." I turned towards the stairs and went inside. I checked in and sat down, barely able to sit still.

I glanced at my phone. No messages. Typical. Whenever someone else is having a crisis, I drop whatever I am doing and help. It's totally comforting to see that the same effort is repaid when I need it. I tossed my phone into my bag and began biting my nails.

I waited for what seemed like an hour before I got called into the back. I sat down in one of the counseling rooms and set my things next to the couch. I played with my thumb, not knowing if I should speak or if she would. She looked over a few details while I waited in silence.

"So," she said addressing me, "how about you start from the beginning."

"It all started about a week ago."

* * *

The sound of my alarm startled me awake. Finding it, I swiped the screen of my phone to silence it.

8:20 is too early for a class, especially Physics. I worked myself up into a seated position, my feet dangling off the side of the bed.

I looked across the room to see an empty bed. I don't know how he does it. He is the last one to bed and the first one to get up. I guess having a disappearing roommate is better than not having one at all. Rubbing the tiredness from my eyes, I slid off the end of the bed to the floor and into the chair in front of my laptop. I opened my email.

Junk. Junk. Junk.

Hmm, chess event in a week? Promising.

I walked over to the chess set on my roommate's desk. I made the first move taking the centermost white pawn and placing it two spaces forward. Going into my drawer, I took out a post-it note and a pen writing, "Your move." I placed it on the opposing side of the board. I grinned and made my way to class.

The walk to Physics was cold and foggy. I was still tired, so it took me awhile to notice, but where was everyone? Classes were going to start soon. I stopped at the top of the stairs to the Science Center and peered through the fog down towards the main road looking for anyone I may have missed.

Leaning against the wall was a man wearing a plaid suit. I could not tell if he was a professor or student. He pointed at me then dropped something on the ground. He walked away, disappearing from my sight behind Perlman Hall. I was moving as quickly as I could without running. Once around the corner, I opened my mouth to ask him where everyone was, but he was gone. I looked up and down the road. Nothing.

I told myself he must have just gone into one of the nearby buildings. I found what he had dropped on the ground—a post-it note that read, "Sure, I'll play. Your move." It took me a minute before it clicked. He was my roommate. I still haven't actually met with him face to face. He moved in about the time Clarence moved out over a month ago. He apparently has an odd sense of style—then again, it is Alfred. We are an eccentric bunch.

I could now see a few people making their way towards their classes. I took out my phone to check the time. Three quarters past seven. I was early this entire time? I opened the alarm on my phone and sure enough, it was set to go off at half past seven instead of the usual alarm I set for eight. Why did I set that alarm? That question nagged me as I walked back up the stairs and into the Science Center.

* * *

I met up with my friends for lunch in Powell. I was working on some math homework at the table when I was interrupted by a waving hand.

"Nathan? Hello? There you are. Welcome back."

I looked up to see my friends staring at me and laughing.

"What?" I asked, raising an eyebrow.

"We were just talking about how lucky you are."

"Yeah, you made out like a bandit."

"Yeah, I would pay for that. My roommate sucks."

I realized they were complaining about their living situations. I never really understood why they were jealous of my roommate. You'd think that having someone living with you would be amazing. Someone who could help you study, someone to talk to, and a possible new friend. Yet all I ever hear my friends say is how inconvenient it is. "Oh yeah, it can be really quiet though. Sometimes I wish someone was there that I could talk to." I turned my attention back towards my math.

"If I wanted that, I would just come and visit you guys."

"I have a girlfriend. Not having a roommate would make life so much easier."

"I might finally be able to study in peace."

I finished the last problem and turned to my friend Leo. "So, are we still on for tonight?"

"Yeah, I was planning on heading out after I finish that homework."

"I just finished mine," I said gesturing to my math papers. "I could help you if you would like."

"Sounds good. Your room around nine? We can be done by ten or eleven and head out after."

"Cool."

Walking towards the third-floor exit, I saw through the glass a familiar figure leaning against one of the support pillars. He looked back at me and held out what looked like another note and dropped it onto the ground in front of him. He took a puff from the cigarette he was holding in his other hand and blew the smoke towards the door obscuring himself from my view. When the smoke cleared, he was gone. Who is he? A magician? Not like I would know—we haven't even talked to each other yet. We always seem to be going in different directions. Either that or he is trying to avoid me. If so, he is doing a brilliant job.

I walked over to where he had been standing and sure enough, on the ground was a post-it note. I picked it up. Written in black sharpie were the words "A party? Good luck." I crumpled it up and looked around to make sure no one was looking over my shoulder. Weird.

* * *

Back in my room I worked on more homework and watched some TV. Thankfully I only have morning classes on Friday. As happy as I was though, the note bothered me. Was he going to tell someone I was going to a party? I walked over to my dresser and pulled out a small balloon full of sand and began to squeeze it.

I barely noticed the next hour pass until I was snapped out of my trance by a loud knocking at the door. "Nathan. Are you going to let me in?" It was Leo.

"Yeah, coming." I let him in.

We began working on the homework. If I am being honest, I barely understood it when I was working through the problems the first time. However, there is one thing I have always believed, if you can teach someone how to do something properly, then you'll know how to do it yourself. I struggled to help him at first, but by the end I felt like I had a better grasp of the concepts. It looked like Leo did too. He made his way over to his backpack and pulled out two bottles. Turning the labels towards me with a grin a mile wide, he whispered, "Pick your poison."

The first bottle was some kind of Vodka I had never heard of. The other some kind of Bourbon. After a moment of indecision, I decided on the Vodka.

"Ah. Vodka," he proclaimed imitating a Russian accent.

* * *

I remember little of what happened that night, but I woke with a splitting headache. I looked over at the chess set and was thoroughly confused. The chess game I had started with my roommate was complete.

Stumbling my way over, I examined the board. I had lost. The game had been very one sided—I took maybe five of his pieces, and three of them were pawns. On my side of the board was a post-it note stating in all capital letters, "YOU LOSE." I was more upset I did not remember seeing my roommate than I was about losing the game. The first chance I had to speak to him and I was too drunk to remember.

I spent the rest of the weekend working on recovering and homework. Buried amongst my assignments was an important essay I had to finish. It was easily worth a quarter of my grade for the course, and I was determined not to fail. It was tough, but I managed to get through it with enough time to still get a good night's sleep.

*　*　*

I woke up to pounding on my door.

"Nathan?" Leo inquired through the door. "Are you alive in there?"

Huh? What is he talking about? I picked up my phone and checked the time. Half past ten. Damn it! How did this happen! I could have sworn that I set an alarm to get me up on time. I scrambled over to my dresser to pick out some clothes as I shouted through the door, "Yeah, I'm alive. My stupid alarm must not have gone off."

"Well you better hurry up unless you want to lose credit for turning in your paper late. I'll see you in class."

*　*　*

When I got to class, I found out my day was only getting worse. When the professor collected the papers, mine was missing. I was looking around frantically when my eyes met my plaid suited roommate in the doorway. He grinned and held up a note that read, "Missing something?" My nostrils flared. That bastard! I got out of my seat as calmly as I could and walked towards the door. His eyes widened and he fled down the hallway.

"Oh no you don't," I said through clenched teeth.

Once I was in the hallway, I took off after him. I followed him around the corner and saw him exit the front doors. I burst through the doors. My eyes darted around wildly looking for him. He was gone. Left with nowhere to direct my anger, I took a swing at a nearby wall. It was a mistake. A sharp pain erupted in my hand.

"Agh!" I growled.

I called the Wellness Center with my good hand. They set me up in a splint and helped me arrange an appointment for x-rays and a cast. By the end of the day, I only had enough energy for one act of anger. I took a out a note and set it on the door to my room. "I am going to inform the school of what you did. I will get you kicked out."

* * *

I didn't see or hear anything from my roommate over the next few days. Everyone wondered what happened to me, but I didn't know how to explain it. When I got back to my room Friday after classes, he was there. Tissues and all my clothes were strewn about the room. I closed the door behind me. There was an odd smell that I couldn't place.

"I thought you had left the school."

He was sitting on his bed still in that stupid plaid suit. He was holding something in his hand. It was a small box of some sort. When he looked up, I saw there were tears running down his face.

I was in no mood to feel sympathy. "This is my room! Get out!"

He struck a match.

* * *

Everyone blamed me for the room fire. I insisted it was my roommate, but no one believed me. I talked to my friends the night it happened. I told them everything. Our game of chess. The notes he left lying around. The plaid suit he always wore. The fact that we partied with him on Friday. At the end of the story, I asked them, "So what do you think?"

My friends gave me a concerned look.

"What is it?" I asked, my heart racing.

"Nathan, you don't have a roommate."

STEREOPTICON, SHOTGUN, BLENDER
SUSAN MOREHOUSE

S OMEDAY, SOON, THE weight of the attic will bring the house down around them. She feels the pressure of things against the back of her neck. In her dream, the destruction of accumulated things begins slowly, as if the weight of a box marked, "Mother's Wedding China, 1950," or "Maternity Clothes – Recycle," will burn through the floor, making a 4x4 hole through which it will fall, landing with a muffled thump on the empty bed in the room beneath it. There it will settle and begin again the process of weight creating heat that burns through quilt and mattress, and so to the floor beneath the bed, and so on, down through the house, past the two of them sitting calmly in the living room reading fiction about other lives as if their own past lives had not reached critical mass.

At first they won't notice, or not enough to do more than look up and say, the way people long-married do in such situations: "Box," shorthand for, "A box has just fallen past, kitchen ware, I think."

It will be like the time he forgot to shut the attic door firmly, and one of the cats fished it open and ended up on the far side of the attic where there is no floor. Such a surprise:

the cat fell through the dropped ceiling previous owners had used to disguise their own fire onto the antique bed in the guest room where he was sleeping. So much dirt on the quilt! Some previous child had plastered glow in the dark stars on the ceiling and now there is a black hole where the Big Dipper used to be.

Meanwhile, the 4x4 hole beckons other boxes filled with other things:

A stereopticon and photos of Niagara Falls, a child's artwork, two saddles, books in several languages, a lace dress of her great grandmother's faded from periwinkle to early cataract blue, Christmas decorations, the fuzzy kind, empty liquor bottles, a chandelier, an overlarge top hat, empty baskets, dead wasps and taxes, a bat in a bag with a blender, crockery and toys, blankets with mouse holes that surely must be good for something, rugs, winter coats, an antique table, a coal stove, a trumpet, and a shotgun with a silver stock.

Strange things, suggesting a life lived by other people somewhere else. She doesn't recognize herself in these things. Soon every box will tilt towards that hole, the larger things falling first and widening it, the way a burn eats slowly at the edges of a piece of wood.

In the living room where they are turning pages, he is reading Trollope and she a romance, they may hear the sounds in the rooms above them. The thunk, thunk, ka-thunk, of so many things, some of them beautiful or valuable but who has the time to sort through the detritus of multiple lives? Things tumble against things, loads shift, there is the crunch of breaking glass like heavy boots on ice in mid-winter. "Did you hear something?" he asks. He has just seen the edge of a box marked "Firsts" falling past in the dining room. His, he thinks.

She sees it, too, but she has reached a good part in the narrative, where the hero and heroine, their lives entirely before them, have just embraced. They are, to use the language of her girlhood, passionately making out. "Did you say something?" she asks.

LIGHTEN UP, DUDE
SYDNEY DOMINICK

"HEY, DUDE, WE did it! My fastest close ever. Told you we'd be out of here quick."

I rolled my eyes and laughed as my shift leader put his hand up for a high five. "Oh, come on, man. It's 11:31. I left at ten past last night." His excited face turned to a scowl. His hand still hanging in the air. A sharp crack rang out and I smiled ignoring the sting in my hand. "Have a good night, man."

As my shift leader set the alarm, I put in my headphones and began my walk home. Snow was falling overhead in dizzying flurries, and for once the bone chilling wind that overcame the town of Alfred during the winter months had stopped. With music in my ears and snow in my hair, I walked towards my dorm. "This couldn't be any better," I whispered to myself.

I came to a dead stop next to a light post on the path that leads back to my building. Frantically, I dug through the mess of receipts, change, and a strange amount of crumbs that were all in my pockets until I found what I was looking for. The night was so silent that anyone within a mile radius would've heard the sound of the impatient flicks of my lighter and seen me exhale with a cloud much too big to simply blame on the cold air. I smiled as I walked and inhaled every time the song I was listening to reached the chorus.

"Now, this couldn't be better." I quickly realized that I didn't whisper this time. Oh well.

I licked my thumb and tamped down the last of the glowing embers as I approached my building. I slipped the remnants back into my pocket. Still enough for tomorrow night's walk home. I went through the side door, started up the stairs, and immediately tripped. Nice. How fucking long have I been walking up these stairs? Oh, hello third floor, good to see you again. Heh. I reached my door and found it unlocked. The light inside was on.

"Hey. How's it going?" I asked with a hint of forced enthusiasm in my voice.

My roommate was sitting on her bed, notebooks strewn everywhere, her eyes glued to her laptop. "Just so you know, you left the lights on when you left for work. If you could make sure they're off next time, that'd be great." Never once did she look up from her laptop or answer my initial question.

"Uh, yeah, sorry about that." I said slowly. I was almost positive that I had turned the lights off when I left. Wait, why did it even matter? What's her problem with me anyway. I never do anyth—

"Hey." Two blue eyes with dark circles under them that hung like drapes peered through the same pair of Walmart glasses my sister had. "Are you good? You keep making the weirdest faces at the popcorn that you seem to be struggling to make."

I was standing next to the microwave holding the unpopped bag, staring off into the distance.

"Yeah, I'm good uh, sorry." I threw the popcorn in the microwave and jumped on my bed.

"Is it cool if I turn out the light soon? My shift kinda sucked. You would not believe—"

"Sure, whatever." Her laptop snapped shut. "I'm actually gonna go to the library for a little. I have some more work to finish."

I was lying on my bed with my knees bent and my hands covering my eyes. "Why, dude, it won't be that dark in here. You have that little night light." I uncovered one of my eyes and looked over at the outlet that had been preoccupied by a heart-shaped night light all semester. It was gone.

"It like died today or something so I threw it out." She began to fill her backpack with all of her things, jumped off her bed, and quickly slipped on her shoes. "Night," she said without looking at me. The normal slam of the door was accompanied by a small explosion consisting of everything that had been propped up against my closet door falling onto the floor. My towel had slipped off the back of my door and triggered said explosion.

"Why, God?" I fake sobbed and catapulted myself off of my bed.

After one look at the mess, I was pretty glad that I was forced to clean it up. A bulletin board. A broom. A sweatshirt that I tried to hang off of the broom. Why didn't I just put this stuff away in the first place? I made some weird shriek at myself and picked up the sweatshirt. Underneath it was more of one man's trash and my own treasure. "Wait. What the fuck?" I laughed. "I can't believe I forgot about this thing." Over winter break my roommate had gone on vacation with her family, and at some point, they went to some zoo or something. While she was in the gift shop, she found one of those weird animal head, claw grabby things? Yeah, that's definitely the official term. Well, she bought me the one that looked like a

Tyrannosaurus Rex because she decided me and Rex had "the same dumb smile."

I put everything back in its upright position against my closet once again. The claw thing was still on the ground, so I picked it up. I stood staring at the toy, opening and closing its mouth over and over again. Turns out I had also been opening and closing my mouth with the toy, and when I finally noticed, I pursed my lips and added it to the pile.

"Ah! My popcorn." I whipped around to my microwave that had been beeping to let me know my snack was done. Popcorn in hand, I attempted to put on pajamas. It didn't occur to me that it would be much easier to put on shorts if I just put the popcorn down for a second. I groaned in frustration at myself and put down my snack. I hopped up on my bed and reached for my laptop. Shoving popcorn into my face, I searched for something to watch. Fuck Netflix right now. "Is crunching popcorn the loudest sound in the world?" I typed into my Google search. After reading quite a few unsatisfactory answers to my question, I finished eating and closed my computer. I stretched my arms high above my head and slapped at the light-switch until the room was dark and silent.

* * *

"Oh fuck." I groaned. I slept through my first class again. As I stumbled out of bed to grab my toothbrush, my phone vibrated against the desk.

A text from my roommate. "The light was on when I came in this morning at like 7am. I don't know why you need it on to sleep???"

I looked up and saw that my roommate's bed was neatly made, and her backpack was gone. I didn't even realize that she hadn't slept here. Why does she care about the goddamn lights so much? I typed quickly as I rolled my eyes. "My bad man."

I shrugged it off and slipped on my flip flops. A shower was just what I needed

* * *

"Hey, check out this weird article."

I stopped staring at the clock and shifted my gaze to the computer next to me. My project partner stared intently at his screen, but not at the lab that we needed to get done in about ten minutes. "Could we just do this, man? Send it to me later and I'll read it after work or something."

"Look, it's short; just read it. It's about Alfred." I wheeled my chair closer to his computer and read the headline: "First Year College Student Found Dead, Roommate Alleged Killer."

"Oh damn," I said with a little surprise. "What year is this from?"

"Looks like uhhhhh…" He scrolled up and down with his mouse quickly. "January 21, 1975," he said finally.

I was already looking at the clock again. Six minutes left. Wait a sec. I furrowed my brow and grabbed the lab I'd been working on. I turned to the first page and looked at the spot next to my name. "Oh snap!" My mouth fell open and I opened my eyes wide as I looked at my partner, trying to look as dramatic as I possibly could. "That's tomorrow!"

He laughed a little, "Did you actually just say 'oh snap?'"

I shook my head and smiled. "Can we get back to this lab. We have one question left and I cannot stay late."

"Alright, alright." He closed out the article. "I just thought you oughta see that 'cause I know how you're roommate gets and I want you to know that someone will write an article with a boring headline about you if you murder her."

I touched my hand to my chest. "I would never." I half closed my eyelids and held up a peace sign with my left hand. "I'm way too chill, man."

We finished up the last question a couple minutes after class had officially ended and I half jogged back to dorm to change into my work clothes. As I slid my key into my lock, I found it already open. Great.

"Hey, dude," I said meekly, not wanting to disturb her. She kept typing whatever she was working on. She didn't respond. I ignored her, sighed, and looked at the clock. Shit, I only had ten minutes until I had to leave for work. Hurriedly, I pulled on my work pants, my shirt, my shoes. My roommate started to put her books in her backpack while I was putting my hair into a ponytail. Why is she fucking leaving if I'm leaving? She's so weird I don't even—

The lights flicked off and she shut the door.

She's lucky I was leaving anyway, or I would have been livid. Scratch that, I was livid. I could feel how red my face was and closed my mouth that had apparently been open since that bitch turned the lights out on me while—

You know what? I don't care. I walked out of my room, locked the door, and flew down the steps.

* * *

"Hey, that was bullshit, what happened in there tonight. If she ever comes in again while you're working, you can step out back for a sec 'til she's gone."

"It's whatever man. The guy behind her tipped like five bucks 'cause he felt so bad, so who cares. Fuck her anyway. Whoever she is, she probably has a way shittier life than me. I hope it made her feel better. Have a good night." I put in my headphones and thrust my hands in my pockets. My hair and shirt smelled like a soured caramel latte. She asked for almond milk. It wasn't on the ticket.

I pulled out a cigarette from a pack that I had found on the floor of a party the weekend before. Fuckin' menthols, man. I smoked two before I figured out that they weren't gonna make my shitty shift any better because, well, it was over. I took the stairs two at a time up to my dorm for no reason.

I stood in the stairwell that lead to my room. My hands pressed together, and my eyes closed. "Please God, if you're up there, please do not let my roommate be in there right now. I'm not gonna promise anything to you in exchange because I'll most likely immediately break it, but yeah."

I went a few doors until I saw those two familiar name tags on the door. Without even putting my keys in, I tried the door. Locked. "Fuck yes," I breathed a sigh of relief, a smile stretched across my face. I slid my hand into my pocket. What the? Where could my keys have gone in less than a minute? I dug through my coat until I realized they were in my back pocket.

I didn't even have them in the door before I heard that condescending but recognizable, "What are you so happy about?"

The smile must have leapt off my face and out the goddamn window because the only thing that I could think to say was, "What are you so unhappy about?" Before my roommate could even respond, I had pushed the door open and thrown off my coat.

"Are you fucking kidding me?" she asked quietly. And then again a little louder. By the third time, she screamed it. "You turned the light on as soon as I turned my back?"

My face contorted and my eyes went blurry. I was quite literally seeing red. "I went to fucking work as soon as you left. I don't have time to play games like you want to. I didn't turn that light on." The words dripped off my tongue like blood off a knife.

"Well this is the first time I've been in here since I left, and oh yeah, I always make sure the light's off when I leave, so."

She pushed past me with a huff and threw her backpack next to her bed. "And you know what, you smell like fucking cigarettes. What, did you run out of weed?" She laughed in the same way that I'm sure she laughed at people she didn't like in high school.

"Dude, how's about growing up? I have done nothing to you ever. Yeah, I smoke, and party, and I leave the fucking light on when I go to the job that I work almost forty-fucking-hours-a-week while also going to school full-fucking-time." I was screaming now, and my fists were clenched. "I didn't leave the fucking lights on tonight." I opened my hands and flexed them by my sides. Then I remembered her text from earlier. "Oh, and I don't think I even left them on last night. No, you know what, I know I turned the lights off because who can sleep with the fucking lights on?"

My roommate was sitting on her bed. I heard the sound of her phone screen shut off and I turned to look at her. Our eyes met for the first time in a while. She sighed a little and cocked her head. "We both know that you were too stoned to even make popcorn. Of course you fell asleep with the light on."

For one single second, all the emotion fell away from my face. I could feel my eyes glaze over, and I relaxed my jaw. "You're right." I laughed a little while I pulled out my ponytail. "You're completely right." I ran my hands through my hair. "I was too fuckin' baked last night to even function. I'm surprised I even woke up this morning, really. I could've sworn I'd be the first person to die of a goddamn marijuana overdose."

Even though I wasn't exactly advocating for the idea that people who smoke weed are level headed and carefree, it didn't stop me from walking around in a circle and yelling all of this shit at the ceiling. Then I noticed the light. The fucking light that at this point had become the bane of my entire existence. Not my roommate, not my job, and not the three papers that I just remembered I have to write for next week, good Christ. I could scream right now. I could just scream and scream and fucking scream and maybe everything would be over, and I could just end this shitty day.

"What the fuck?" A low whisper came from the direction of my roommate's bed.

The look on her face must've been something. I say must've been because I couldn't exactly see it. I couldn't see anything actually. I could, however, feel pieces of plastic? Glass? I'm not entirely sure what it was, but it was stuck in my hair and crunched around my feet as I stepped backwards. "Guess I can't leave it on now."

The air in the dorm was thick with contempt. Neither of us moved. Neither of us bothered to turn on a flashlight. We just remained frozen, both coming to terms with what I had just done. When my head had stopped spinning, I turned to look at the only light in the room. The time on the microwave read 12:06 a.m.

I rubbed my eyes and listened to the nervous flicking of a light switch. "Are you serious, dude? The light's not gonna work right now."

"It's not me," my roommate whispered barely louder than we were breathing.

The flicking didn't stop. It grew faster, and faster, and faster until I heard a hand slip off the switch itself, and a panicked sob emerged from the darkness. I steadied myself and pulled my phone out of my coat pocket. With one deep breath I clicked on the flashlight in the direction of the light switch. A pale face stared back at me.

Its dark hair moved in wisps and the mouth trembled. "I—I don't like to be in the dark. Please don't leave me in the dark. My roommate wanted to keep me in the dark too."

I turned away from this, this figure and looked back at my roommate. I could just barely make out her face because the light from my phone was casting all types of shadows on the remainder of the room. She was unmoving, in shock, horror. With the shadows, she was comparable to the statues of furies that you see when you learn about Greek mythology in middle school. I had only turned around to see my roommate for a second, no, half a second, and when I turned back, the figure was gone. Wait, where the fuck?

My mind stopped completely. I don't know how long I stood there until my blood could completely thaw. "Um." I said out loud. It was the only thing I could think. My heart beat louder than any thought I had.

"Um," I said again. I was staring at the broken light. "Hey, um. You wanna like, take a ride to Dollar General? I kinda miss havin' that night light in here."

My roommate's body relaxed a bit. I don't think I've ever seen her do that before. Her face was still pretty white though, like she'd seen a ghost or something. "Uh." She stopped short with a quizzical expression. "I think Dollar General is closed. We can go to Wegman's though. Want me to drive?"

"Sounds good, man. Let's go." I started to put my phone in my pocket.

"Oh, wait." I pulled my hand back out. The flashlight was still on when I reached for my phone charger. As I began to plug in my phone, I realized I still had something in my hand other hand.

"Seriously?" My roommate choked on a laugh. "That's what you fucking smashed that light out with? That's the last time I get you a present."

All of a sudden, we both were laughing hysterically. I swear to God I almost pissed myself, and I could see tears coming out of my roommate's eyes. I looked at what I was holding one more time. The face of the Tyrannosaurus looked back at me smirking. Huh, I guess we did have the same smile. I threw the toy onto my bed and admired how his prehistoric face was illuminated by the light of my phone. I smiled and shook my head.

"Fuckin' Christ, man." I ran both hands through my hair as we walked out the door.

THE MIRROR
MEGHAN RAHNER

THE BRICK WAS a beautiful old thing with its never-ending staircases and creaky paneled floors. I admired its character, even the musty smell. I have always loved old things. When I was younger, I collected cloth dolls from local antique stores. They smelled like sawdust and had faded yarn hair. I used to line them all up in a row next to my bed, but I covered their faces with tissues while I slept. I did not want them watching me.

I worked at The Brick as a Resident Assistant. In order to make the building presentable for the students, I took a surveyed the halls and hung nametags on doors. The staircases were beautiful with wooden carvings of bats and grainy textures. I followed the carvings that spiraled and transcended up the railings. The air got heavier with each floor, and the lighting dimmed. The electrician must have run out of the good bulbs after the first floor.

The hallways were laid out in a "T" formation to maximize the space. On the third floor, adorned in the corner of the hallway, I discovered a yellow, faded full length mirror. It had a ram's head carved into the top of its frame. The horns curled over the glass and gave my reflection a crown. Each room already came equipped with a mirror, and yet here it stood. I yanked at its sides, but it would not budge. The mirror was mounted to the building's woodwork. Some crazy architect must have been really drunk. Not that odd architecture was bad; there was a unique beauty to it.

I stopped pulling to look at my reflection. My nose carried itself straight despite my breaking it four times. My eyes seemed carved into my face with their bright hazel. Other girls got nose jobs and Botox and cut off the pieces they found undesirable. Was I pretty? What did people think when they saw me? In grade school there was a girl called Morgana, like the sorceress in the King Arthur tales. All of the guys thought she was the prettiest in the school because she had highlights in her hair and a fake tan. She teased me for my frizzy hair and blemished skin. I stepped closer to the mirror to inspect my skin, and something twitched in my reflection. My fingers ran down the reflective surface, stroking it. The surface felt smooth and cold. A beautiful old thing.

The day before residents moved in, I joined with my other RAs for a staff meeting. I mentioned the mirror, and they said they had seen it but then waved me off. The group drooped from the day's training, so I dropped the subject.

That night the old building creaked whenever the wind decided to reach its tendrils into the hollow walls, but I did eventually sleep. The wind became my friend and came into the building to find me. Like a game of hide and seek. I dreamed the mirror turned into a portal filled with orange wisps of fire. Stepping into the opening, a black gravel path lined with blooming rhododendrons appeared in front of me. Ahead, a crimson sky curled its clouds into a smile. I kept dashing ahead, faster and faster, but suddenly a split in the road appeared and I lurched to a halt.

Waking up the next morning, I felt sore, and my water bottle had disappeared from my nightstand. I saw it hanging from a rusty hook in the closet. Ever since age three, I tended to sleep walk. Mama told me stories where she would find me wandering throughout the house with eyes open, but completely unaware. She guided me back to my bed and tucked me in with a kiss. The mornings after, sometimes I remembered the incidents as if I had dreamed them, but sometimes I remembered nothing at all.

My sisters teased me whenever they found out. "You're possessed, you freak!"

Mama scolded them when they stepped out of line. Mama protected the family.

I dressed and went to meet the new residents. As they arrived, I smiled and gave them their shiny new keys. "Hello, I am your RA, Cleo. Let me know if you need anything."

The responses were mostly positive with many "nice to meet yous" and "thank yous." A few gave suspicious glares. I could hear them thinking, "I know your kind—you smile at first, but then report us later."

People are confusing. They use their eyes too much when they need to use their brains. Mama always said not to let people see you're afraid, or they will hunt you down and take your happiness. I wouldn't let the new residents take mine.

Later, I rushed around to each room and tried to make conversation with as many people as I could. People like it when they get compliments. "I love your shirt! Where did you get it?"

"Oh, thank you! It was a present from one of my friends. I like your shirt too!"

Two of the residents, however, leered like rattlesnakes. Two boys with wide eyes. The usual human conversation did not work with them. They sneered at every attempt I made to be friendly. They seemed to be the calculating type. They squinted and searched my face with their suspicious eyes. It was best to leave them be as much as possible.

That night the mirror portal came again in my sleep. The crossroads still remained. They mocked me. They whispered, "Choose, little one!"

But once again I couldn't. It was like choosing which arm to cut off.

The following morning, I ran to my meeting with the head of Residence Life. I heard rumors that the administrators could be cruel and unreasonable, but so far nothing led me to suspect they were. All the same, I did not want to be late. Julie, the head administrator, met with me. She had swampy green hair that she flipped over her shoulder when she became irritated. The green hair was a mystery. I suppose she thought it looked edgy and fashion forward, but it resulted in a more alien than human display. She pierced me with her judgmental gaze and asked about my plans for doing the job well. She was as inviting as a porcupine.

I replied that I simply would work very hard. She gave an approving nod and set up another meeting for the next week. She handed over some posters for a theater production to put up around my hall. I left with my spine still feeling nettlesome. She gave no indication of displeasure, but showed that she preferred to be in a hot bath with a glass of chardonnay than around immature college students.

Stiffness like a knife in my side greeted me when I got up the next morning. Exhaustion and stress does that to you. Either that or the ungodly hard bed. Today, I had a hall meeting with the residents. Some of them had been using the bathroom sink as their personal garbage disposal. The cleaning lady found waxing strips, ramen, and hair in the girls' bathroom the day before. I pulled myself from the grasping arms of my covers. There was a new bruise on my elbow and one on my calf. Stupid hard bed.

In high school, Morgana wore outfits to impress the teenage boys. A pair of tight jeans that made her butt look good, a clean form-fitting tee-shirt and a distressed denim jacket always got the boys gazing. My outfits were somewhat less appealing. In the closet hung a spotted blouse and a dark pair of jeans. It's not the best, but good enough. I dressed and went to look at myself in the third-floor mirror. The outfit didn't look bad when my image was framed by the mirror. The mirror was a charmer. It flattered me until I blushed. "Everyone will love you in this outfit. They will look at you and they will love you, or they will hate you if they don't like your face."

It was challenging walking down the stairs. My heart faltered thinking about all the residents' faces, their eyes looking deep inside me and taking my happiness. The weight of being judged crushed my chest with every step. A snowball formed inside my brain. It rolled over and over and gained momentum. The heaviness of my chest became greater and the snowball larger. It rolled through every insecure thought, picked them up and mashed them all together: ugliness, stupidity, hatred. Faster and faster. Rolling. Then, on the bottom step, it shattered. I can do this; no fear. The attentive resident faces emerged, and I gave the meeting.

Many of the residents seemed very pleased. They smiled and politely agreed to clean up their future messes. No devastation. An avalanche avoided for today. To celebrate, I thought it would be nice to look at my friend, the mirror. When I arrived, the two boys with the wide eyes were blocking the view as they stared into the mirror themselves. They smiled subtly and then turned their eyes towards me. How dare they try to take my mirror from me! When they looked at me, they stared blankly. The reflection of their faces twitched—a slight smirk—and then they went down the staircase.

As soon as their heads vanished beneath the carving of the banister, the mirror seemed brighter than ever and beckoning. Resistance felt impossible. I rushed and grasped the mirror in my hands. It whispered to me like an old lover. The glass started to fog from my breath, so I wrote my name in it.

That night the two pathways came before me again. Which to choose? The crimson sun was scorching, and the air tasted of fried fish. Suddenly, a tearing sensation ripped through the middle of my body. It was painful, but also felt like the release of chains. The knots loosened, and everything felt open and clear.

For the weeks that followed, I fell into a solid routine: wake up, classes, homework, gaze at the mirror, bed. The days fell into a blur. The mirror dreams stopped, but some mornings I found objects were moved around in the room. Other times, an outfit lay out on the chair; normal sleepwalking occurrences. Most of the time, everything was mundane. Then, at one of the meetings with Julie, she mentioned the boys with the wide eyes. She said they didn't like me, and they wanted me removed. Of course, they wanted my mirror. They didn't care where I stayed as long as they got the mirror.

Julie said, "Of course you are just doing your job, so no need to fret. I'm sure they will get over whatever problems they are having. It's all a silly misunderstanding. I mean, who would believe their ridiculous stories. You threatening them with a spoon? And screaming about a mirror? It's poppycock. Just carry on."

Maybe the stress of this job got to me. The late nights on call and the constant social anxiety could not be brushed off. Just all those people staring and judging and then you trying to figure out what you did wrong. Think reasonably about this. Don't do anything stupid. You need to keep this job. I smoothed down my hair and told Julie that I wouldn't worry about it too much. She mentioned, "Hey hun, maybe it would be better if you tried to be friendlier to the residents. An RA can be intimidating, so maybe being friendlier would make you less of a threat. I think you need to try harder. Sound good, hun?" An order not a request.

I grunted in compliance and left quickly. I relished being free of her alien presence. Her words seemed reasonable, but her demeanor reeked of insensitivity. Last semester, one Resident Assistant told her that residents were spitting and throwing eggs at her door, but Julie did nothing. She never wanted to hear the problems. All she ever said was to do better.

That night I lay awake thinking as I stared at the water-damaged panel on the ceiling. It was hard to read people, to understand what they wanted. I couldn't figure out what to say. Each word, a consequence. Each sentence, multiple meanings. Each conversation could lead to an undesired outcome. Roots started to grow with every thought. They twisted in and out of each other. The vines reached up into the image of my mother telling me, "Don't trust them—they crave your destruction." The roots needed to be cut to let me breathe again. All the exhausting thoughts made it impossible to keep conscious. My vision gave out and darkness came.

That night was no different from the nights before, except for the awakening. That morning everything was out of place. Not messy, but like someone had rearranged the room to their preference. My dresser pushed the door closed and my desk lay perpendicular to my bed. A full outfit lay out on one of the chairs, underwear and all, perfectly coordinated. "What the heck? I might as well wear it. Thanks, dream me."

It was a wool sweater with stripes on one side and flowers on the other, a pair of dark jeans, and rose-colored ballet flats. I dressed and went to roam the hallways. I found myself at the mirror, but something changed. Something written in the glass. I stepped closer and the reflected sunlight blinded me for a moment. Then, the letters came into view: "Why do they look at you?" At this moment, my eyes opened, and I saw in the mirror two faces twitching. Two minds, one person. Another person inside my body. It was the other face talking the entire time.

She scratched those letters on the mirror to make me realize what everyone had done to me. Julie, demanding the world of me, residents, judging my actions and appearance, and the two boys, mocking me. Turning back to her reflection, she gestured forward, beckoning me into her world. I suppose it's better than staying here. I attempted to put my foot through the glass, but the portal didn't want to let me in. I shoved harder and crunched my toes against the surface. Eventually, I had to kick and thrash against the glass to gain any headway at all. A final kick made an entry point for me, but just as I

started to step through, the two boys came running up the
stairs. When they saw me, their faces froze, and their eyes widened. One of them pointed at me. I looked down. My hands
and feet were covered in blood.

THE MORTICIAN
MEGHAN RAHNER

HOW CAN ONE man be so insignificant and yet have such an impact in passing? The faint of heart couldn't endure his occupation. The doctor took the lifeless bodies and made them beautiful. The mothers and fathers always responded with gratitude. They smiled and cried when they saw his work.

Children feared to go near his workroom. It reeked of formaldehyde. The tools around the room shone so brightly that even the heavens could see them. Tap, tap, tap. Each tool clattered back and forth from the metal tray to his masterpiece. Such meticulous work, it takes steady hands. "Hands that are useful for tying knots," I thought.

The doctor appeared in town out of nowhere. No one knew where he came from or who he used to be. His acquaintances few, but his friends even fewer. He stiffness in conversation resembled the stiffness of his subjects. He started each sentence with "Ehs" and "Ers" which led to his interest in uncomfortable subjects like the classification of the internal organs and which substances turned the liver green. Maybe some would find it fascinating, but to us, it was grotesque.

The doctor did, however, have another area of interest. Miss May, the school teacher, who cared for everyone she came across and had hair so beautiful that a crow might pluck it from her head to carry it back to her nest as a prize. On the weekends, she volunteered as a nurse at the infirmary in The Brick. The wounded perked up when they saw her smiling face. She peaked the doctor's interest, and he watched her through the fogging windows of his shop as she made her way to the school house. He craved her. Sometimes days would pass without seeing her, but still he stayed by the window, waiting to catch a glimpse of her again.

 Some days, she took walks to the drugstore to chat with Achie Swib, the baker boy. He made jokes and she blushed and giggled back. The doctor watched their exchanges from a bench outside, holding a paper up to his face to avoid suspicion. If Miss May gave Achie a kiss, the doctor's knuckles turned white.

Twice the doctor tried to send flowers to her door, but as soon as she heard who they were from, she rejected them. Eventually, he learned to send the flowers under the name of the Archie Swib. She gladly accepted them from the florist. He even snuck love notes into the bouquets professing his admiration for her tiny waist and delicious lips. He said her physique was one of the best specimens he had ever seen, and he drew it often while watching from the bench.

However, she did not love him. The doctor's dark demeanor only cast a shadow on her rays of sunlight. She found her joy elsewhere, often with the children. Sometimes she frolicked with Charlie, the paper boy, out in the meadows of Mildred's field, and sang nursery rhymes about cats and unicorns. Her sunshine could have saved him.

* * *

Miss Tophet, the Town Hall secretary, discovered the doctor on her stroll past his workplace. His bulging eyes and dangling feet made her fall into hysterics. Ricocheting down the lane, she reached Constable Barns. It took all his intellect to understand her babbling, but when he did, he rushed to the scene.

Preparing the body became an easy task because his work table already possessed the correct tools and chemicals. No one came to the funeral perhaps because the doctor's life lacked luster or simply wasn't worth the time. I do not know if anyone visited the grave. His isolation defined him in both life and death. Miss May wandered past the stone a few times out of curiosity, but no one else cared.

Four nights past after the funeral, and a cloudy silhouette arose behind Miss May on one of her walks to the drug store. She did not detect the figure lurking behind her. The baker boy saw it and cried out, but the figure did not respond.

Furious, the baker boy barged up. "Hey, you! Did you not hear me, creep?"

A set of protuberant eyes pulled themselves up into a crazed skull and glared. Then the figure turned back and continued along its way. Miss May, seemingly unfazed, continued on her walk.

The town of Alfred now has a reputation. It's hard to decide if it is a good or bad one, but it draws scientists and sceptics from all over. They poke in every cranny and examine every person, but no explanation ever surfaces. No one knows if the figure was real or a ghost. Miss May never married even though Archie Swib asked her many times. Maybe she felt pity for the doctor, or guilt over his death. However, if you catch a glimpse of her sitting room, she keeps not one, but two rocking chairs. Sometimes you can see one rocking slowly, gently, as if occupied by a contented soul.

WHY SHOULD I CARE WHO DIED?
JOSHUA BENHAM

SOMEONE IS DEAD and Powell Campus Center is closed.

That was all the information given to students Sunday morning after it happened. At any college, a death on campus is a big deal, but even more so at a school as small as Alfred University. The president of the university announced through email that more information would be forthcoming and that students should not speculate or spread misinformation. So naturally, that's all my friends did the following day at lunch.

"Did you hear what happened?"

"Yeah, everyone's talking about it."

"I heard it was a student."

"That she fell down the stairs."

"No, no it was the janitor."

"Yeah, he mixed some chemicals wrong and suffocated."

"No, I mean he was the one that did it."

"I heard he killed an A-State student that broke in."

"No one from A-State died. It was a student here I'm sure."

"I just hope Powell is open again this Saturday. I can't bear the thought of Ade being open on the weekend." I didn't mean to say it out loud, but that was the issue weighing on my mind. Between the two meal options on campus, I much preferred Powell. Sure it's tragic that someone died, but by now I would have noticed if it was someone important to me. So really this whole situation was old news. The rumors and incessant chatter of the entire student body was beginning to irritate me. I just wanted to focus on the future. I have two exams this week.

My friends did not share the same sentiments. Instead, they looked at me as if I suggested we go grave robbing this weekend. The table fell silent. I shuffled uncomfortably in my seat as their eyes drilled into me. No one said a word. Compared to the noise of the dining hall around us, the quiet was unsettling.

"Surely we've all been thinking it?" I said, breaking the silence. "We hate eating at Ade. The only reason we're here right now is because Powell's closed." I finished my statement, securing my position of defiance against the larger group. I hoped someone would pity me and take my side. But when the silence returned, I knew that my friends had forgotten their compassion. I felt backed into a corner. I couldn't go back on what I said. Rather than defend myself in vain, I decided to escape the situation.

"I'll uh—I'll see you guys later," I stammered as I hastily gathered my dirty dishes and left the table. As soon as I left, I could hear my friends continue their conversation, likely talking about how insensitive they think I am. The thought turned my defiance to anger. Who needs them anyway?

* * *

I spent the rest of the day alone.

None of my afternoon classes contained any of my friends, which was fortunate because I didn't particularly want to see them after our unpleasant lunch. I skipped dinner partially for the same reason, but I also felt nauseous. Ade food always did make me sick.

After sunset, I walked by Powell as I returned to my dorm. The lights in the building were on. It seemed a bit late to be investigating the scene of a death. Or cleaning, I thought as I remembered the rumors of janitorial murder from earlier. I put the gory mental image aside and quickened my pace. As I ascended the hill running parallel with the building, a flash of movement in a second-floor window caught my eye. I stopped and turned towards the building, scanning all visible windows for the flash's return. My patience was rewarded with the appearance of a humanoid shape in the next window over. The body stopped moving the instant my eyes locked on it. I stood, mesmerized, as the figure faced the window and looked out. The face scanned the surrounding area. It appeared to be a man with a twisted-up kind of expression. As far as I knew, I was the only person on the hill right now. It was only a matter of time before the man spotted me.

Then, seemingly content with his examination of the hillside, the man turned away from the window and walked off, disappearing from view. Did he see me? I don't know how long I spent looking for a glimpse of that face again, but it never appeared. The lights in the building turned off suddenly, room by room. The hillside felt darker without the ambient light from Powell. I shivered as a gust of wind blew across me, and I remembered my initial goal of returning to the light and warmth of my dorm room. I dropped my head to protect my face from the wind. I took all of two steps before I found my path impeded by someone. My eyes locked with those of a young woman. I jumped back, almost slipping on the snow. The woman merely cocked her head.

"Did you see him too? In the window I mean?" she whispered.

"Jesus what the hell do you think you're doing sneaking up on someone like that?" I shouted.

She flinched but stood her ground. She still looked at me directly in the eyes. "I was worried I was the only one who could see him. I saw you stop and stare at the building, so I just had to ask. You saw the man in the window?" She looked at me eagerly.

"I saw *a* man in the window. He was probably—"

"Which window? Was it that one?" She pointed with her finger without looking away from me. Sure enough, she was pointing at the window the man's face had appeared in.

"Yeah, it was that window. How'd you know?"

At my words, the girl sighed with relief. "Oh, thank god. I thought I was losing my mind. When I heard about the death in Powell yesterday, I came by to see if I could find anything out. The cops wouldn't let me in, of course, but while leaving I saw the man in the window. He looked right at me, and then he disappeared. No one around me noticed anything, but I have a feeling that something's up. What do you know about what happened?"

"I—I don't know anything really, just what the email said. I don't even know who died," I replied, caught off guard by her sudden bombardment of words. A sudden thought came into my head. "Do you know who it was?"

The girl didn't respond. For the first time, her eyes wandered away from my face. She looked towards Powell and sighed. I realized the gravity of what I had asked this complete stranger.

"I'm sorry—I didn't mean to—Ah, I mean, I didn't know, did I?" I stammered.

She turned back to me. When our eyes met, it felt like I saw her for the first time. She had stopped staring at me, and her face was no longer exaggerated by the darkness around us and the adrenaline from my surprise. "No, nothing certain. There are just some people I haven't seen or talked to since last week. Don't worry about it."

"Well, maybe they were just really busy this weekend? That happens from time to time," I offered.

At first, I thought she found my words comforting, but as her face hardened into a scowl I could tell my words were less than helpful. "This isn't some game of hide and seek. Somebody died in there. I'm worried about what happened. Don't you care at all?"

"I'm just trying to be realistic. College students get busy. I'm just trying to help you feel better," I retorted.

"If you want to help me feel better, you could do more than just stand there acting like a jerk." Her voice started to rise.

"Why on earth would I help you? I don't even know who you are!" I raised my voice to match hers.

"My name's Mary. Now you know who I am. There's something going on and you're the only other one who's seen anything."

"You're nuts! There's nothing going on here. Someone died and that's tragic but that doesn't mean there's some conspiracy going on, or that it's my problem!"

I pushed past her and walked up the hill, not stopping when she shouted after me, "Wait, stop! You have to help me! Please!"

I didn't look back, and after a few moments, she fell silent. Worried she was following me, I turned back. But she had vanished. Had she really given up and left already? The wind chilled me again, so I decided to leave my speculating for when I'm inside. As usual, my roommate was out when I arrived, so I had the room to myself. I attempted some homework but soon gave up and started watching The Office on my computer.

After watching a few more episodes than I had anticipated, I decided to go to bed. As I lay down in the dark trying to sleep, my mind wandered back to Powell. I told that woman—Mary—that nothing weird was going on and that I wouldn't help her. But the look on that man's face. Why couldn't I look away from it? Why was he even in there? He could be a janitor or someone shutting down Powell for the night, but that doesn't explain his examination of the hillside. Despite all these thoughts, I eventually fell asleep, and my dreams were filled with images of the man's contorted face and Mary's piercing stare.

* * *

Powell did not open on Tuesday.

People were already losing interest. I overheard fewer discussions about the theorized murder/accident. I wondered if my friends had started to understand my disinterest in this whole affair yet. Although I missed eating meals with them, I didn't want them trying to force an apology out of me, so I ate alone.

"Mind if I join you?" a strange but familiar voice said.

I turned and was greeted with Mary's intense stare. I had been hoping all day that I had dreamed up the events from last night, but with her appearance the reality of yesterday was confirmed. "What, are you following me now? I already told you I won't help you."

"Please, just give me a few minutes. I wanted to apologize for my behavior last night," she said, moving quickly to get back within eyesight of me.

I raised my eyebrows. "I don't know, I'm pretty busy right now." I refused to meet her gaze.

"What? Busy spying on that table over there?" she said callously, pointing at the table my friends were sitting at. I didn't consciously know I was doing it, but at her words I realized I had been eavesdropping since my arrival. It made me pause. Mary smiled and continued speaking, "You were being pretty obvious about it. Maybe I should go tell them that they've got a shadow."

"Alright, you can stay, but make it quick," I said. I gestured for her to sit down, but she had already seated herself. I noticed that she had no food with her. "Aren't you going to eat anything?"

"No, I'm not very hungry right now. Can't really stand Ade food, to be honest."

"Yeah, me neither," I said. Not wanting to bring up Powell unnecessarily after everything that happened yesterday, I resisted the urge to say more. Suddenly, she chuckled to herself. "What's so funny?"

"I just realized I don't actually know your name." She was laughing now.

I couldn't help but smirk at this oversight. "Well, that does put a bit of a damper on things, doesn't it. I'm Alex." The moment of humor passed, and we sat in an uncomfortable silence. Tired of waiting for something to happen, I spoke. "What did you want to talk about anyways?"

"I just wanted to apologize for being so rude last night. I was worried about what happened, and I took it out on you. So, I'm sorry."

"I understand. I had a pretty crappy day too, so that's why I wasn't in the best mood to talk to a stranger," I responded. I had treated her just as poorly, if not more so. "I'm sorry too."

"Apology accepted. Let's just start over fresh. So you saw the man in the window? Dark hair, angry looking?"

"Yeah I did. He was in the window you pointed at. All the lights in the building went out. Then you showed up. That's really all I know." I wondered how she thought I could be helpful at all. "What about you? Do you know anything?"

"Just what the email said, mostly." I waited for her to say more, but that was it.

"Oh come on, you said last night you had some theories. What are they?"

"Just some ideas based on people I haven't seen in a while. But it could really be anyone. I just worry a lot."

"Like who?" I asked without thinking. The second the words left my mouth, I knew I had repeated my mistake from last night.

Mary's head drooped as she thought about the answer to my question. Then, she laughed to herself again. This time, though, it sounded a little different. "You sure ask a lot of questions for someone who claims this 'isn't your problem,'" she said, speaking the last few works in an impression of my voice so bad I hoped it was intentional. I took the jab as atonement for my blunder. We looked at each other for a moment. "Okay, okay. I'm mostly worried about my friend, Sarah. We had a bit of a fight on Friday and I haven't seen or heard from her since. You don't know any Sarahs, do you?"

"I'm afraid not, sorry." Before we dwelled on unpleasant hypotheticals about Sarah for too long, I changed the subject. "What about the guy in the window? Know anything about him?"

"I've never seen him before. I spend a lot of time in Powell, but the first time I saw him was after the death. A cop maybe? Someone investigating? I'm not sure. But I have to know more."

"Why don't we go back to Powell tonight and investigate some more?" I proposed.

Mary looked as shocked as I felt. Seeing her face as she thought of what might have happened though, I just had to do something. While the sadness was not completely gone, a light returned to her eyes. "Do you mean it? You'll help me?"

I realized I might regret offering my help, but I couldn't take back what I said. "Yeah, I'll help. I have some work to do tonight, but afterwards we can meet at the King Alfred statue."

"Oh, thank you, Alex!" She pulled her phone out of her pocket and offered it to me. "Here, put your phone number down. I'll text you when I'm headed to the statue."

I took it and, somewhat reluctantly, put my name and phone number into a new contact. She reclaimed her phone and examined what I had entered. She started typing and, from the other side of the table, I could see that she was changing my name.

"Hey what are you—," I began before I noticed what she was doing. She was changing my name to Jerk. "Come on, Mary, I thought we were past that?"

"I know a million people named Alex," she said, smiling wickedly. "This way, I definitely won't forget you. See you tonight, jerk."

* * *

What did I get myself into?

She texted me later that night. I ignored her for several minutes, but I made a promise so I agreed to meet her at the King Alfred statue at eight o'clock. The time passed too quickly and before I knew it, I had to leave the comfort and normalcy of my room. I sighed as I stood up from my bed and made my way out of the building.

I saw her standing at the statue, shivering in the cold. She was looking around, likely for me. I felt an incredible urge to sneak up on her and frighten her, but I didn't want to do anything else to deserve my jerk title. I called out to her from a distance and completed my approach as she turned and greeted me. "So, what do you think we should try?" I asked her. "Powell is going to be locked and we can't exactly break in."

"I suppose to start we could look through the doors on the second-floor entrance," Mary responded after thinking for a moment. "Maybe we can see if there's anything weird near the window we saw the man in."

We walked towards the building along a path that led directly to the second-floor entrance. I peered through the glass door, cupping my hands around my eyes to block out the light coming from the lamps around us. Being near the building did not make it any less dark inside, but before I could ask Mary how she expected us to see anything, I saw the beam of a flashlight illuminating a small section of the interior.

Powell looked the same as always. The same chairs, tables, and help desk all resided in their normal places. When Mary shone her flashlight at the right angle, I could see through the glass panel on the far wall into the bookstore. At another angle, I could see the stairs going up to the third floor on my right. Nothing seemed out of place at all.

"Do you see anything?" Mary asked.

"No, nothing. Although the window that I saw the man in is over to the left more, the wall is blocking it. This isn't a good angle. We won't see anything here." As I spoke, something caught the corner of my eye. It moved near the back wall, but I couldn't remember seeing anything out of the ordinary there. "Wait, Mary, stop moving the flashlight for a second. Can you shine it over there?"

After I indicated to her where I saw the movement, I learned I had merely been tricked by the low light. There was only a glossy poster on the wall. Mary sighed when she realized there was nothing interesting to see.

"Sorry, it must have been a trick of the light," I said. "I didn't sleep much last night, so I guess I'm getting fooled pretty easily. Maybe we missed something. Let's look for a little longer."

She turned her face back towards the glass door, signaling her agreement. I followed suit and began a second examination of the entrance area. This time around, something looked off, but I couldn't figure out what it was. I heard a quiet click next to me as Mary turned off her flashlight and I knew immediately what was different.

"Do you see it too?" I asked, already knowing the answer.

"Was it always there?"

"No, it must have been while we were looking at the poster."

We were both looking at the staircase to the third floor. A very dim light emanated from the third floor. It lit up the stairs and a small area of the floor around the first step. It was so faint we almost couldn't see it when the flashlight was on.

"Where do you think it's coming from, Alex?"

"I don't know, but we could probably see it through the doors up on the third floor. Let's hurry, before it goes out." I broke away from the door first and Mary followed. I took the path running next to the building up the hill, pushing my way through unshoveled snow.

"Alex! Wait for me!" I turned and saw her struggling to maneuver through the shin-deep snow. I returned to her, mostly sliding, and took her hand. I practically pulled her up the hill. We made it to the back of the building, covered in snow from a single fall. We ran to the doors and pushed our faces against the freezing glass. The inside of the building was dark again. The light was gone.

"Where'd it go? Do you see anything?"

"No, nothing. But I saw light, I swear." We scanned the dark hallway and the adjacent stairs, looking in vain for the light that brought us up here. The light was dim, but if it was coming from up here, we would have seen it by now. I turned away from the door. "Mary, I don't think we'll see anything else here and I'm starting to lose feeling in my fingers. Maybe we should go before we get too cold. I'm sorry we didn't find anything useful."

"No, there has to be something here. We saw it," Mary said, continuing to look through the glass. "There has to be."

I turned back to her. She was shivering, and, even in the low campus lighting, I could see that her face was incredibly pale. I took her arm and tried to turn her away from the door, but she resisted. I abandoned the attempt and walked away from Powell, with the intent of leaving Mary to her search alone. I stopped when I heard her call out to me.

"Alex, look! The light is back! It's coming from the wall!"

I rushed back to her. I slid on the ice as I tried to stop and gave the door a solid headbutt. I ignored the throbbing pain in my head as I peered through the door. The hallway was now illuminated in a dim light that spilled over the railing on the steps. It was the same light as before. It emanated from a recess on the right side of the hallway. The elevator. On the floor of the hallway, a clear shadow also originated from the elevator. Someone was inside.

"I don't understand. The building is closed. Who could be using the elevator?" I asked. Mary did not respond. We studied the hallway in silence. The shadow shifted slightly. I felt a strong urge to run away, but I couldn't avert my eyes.

"You saw it move too, right?" Mary asked me. I almost couldn't hear her. Before I could respond, the shadow moved again, and I saw the figure of a man walk out of the elevator. The pain in my head intensified when he appeared. I felt Mary grab my hand, squeezing it very tightly. The man turned his head towards us. It was the same face I had seen in the window. Our eyes met and I jumped back. I slid on the ice again and fell backwards, pulling Mary down with me. She landed on top of me, forcing all the breath from my lungs. We scrambled to sit up, but by the time we looked back through the door, both the man and the light were gone.

* * *

We didn't see anything else that night and went our separate ways. My dreams were filled with nightmares of the man from the window. He was chasing me, but no matter how fast I ran, he was always the same distance away from me, walking slowly, almost casually.

My head screamed with pain when the vibration of my phone woke me up. After a few moments, the sensation faded and I could see that Mary had called me. Rubbing the sleep from my eyes, I listened to the voicemail she left me:

"Alex! It's Mary! Great news! Sarah's okay! She finally responded to all of my messages. She had gone home for the weekend and her phone broke after she left it in her sweatshirt and washed it. And when her parents heard about the death, they didn't want to bring her back on campus until they knew it was safe. She'll be coming back later today. Oh, I'm so relieved. I can't believe I didn't think to email her. But anyways,

I just wanted to let you know that everything's all good now, so you're off the hook, jerk ha-ha… Unless, of course, you want to keep investigating with me. Last night was kind of… exhilarating and I want to know more. I was really glad to have someone with me, so let me know, okay? All right, bye."

Being so early in the morning, it took me a few minutes to process all of that information. Mary's friend was safe, and she said I could stop looking into the man in the window. After my nightmare last night, I was in no rush to see that face again. But to let Mary keep investigating on her own? I could tell that man was dangerous from the way he looked at me both last night and when I first saw him. Whoever he was, he could hurt me. He could hurt Mary. She'd only ever talked to me because I had seen him. Would that stop now that I wasn't a part of the search?

"Let's eat lunch together again and talk things over," I texted her. Within a few minutes she replied with an affirmation and I carried on with my morning.

* * *

I arrived at Ade before Mary. Some of my friends were already inside. I could see them watch me out of the corners of their eyes as I walked past their table. When I had made it clear that I wasn't going to sit with them, they resumed their conversation. Mary arrived within ten minutes and joined me with her lunch.

"I'm glad your friend is all right."

"Yeah, me too. I was getting really worried. So, what did you want to talk about? Do you not want to keep up the search?" Mary asked between mouthfuls of pizza made with a sauce that smelled much too sweet.

"I just think now that we know your friend is safe, there really isn't a need to try to find out things on our own. I'm sure there's an investigation going on, and we could get into a lot of trouble for interfering."

"But don't you want to know? Why was that man there all by himself last night? Who actually died? There's something weird going on here. Aren't you curious?"

"I mean, yeah. I want to know, but I don't even know what else there is we can do short of breaking into Powell. And that man. I don't think he's someone we want to meet again. Something seems off about him. Something bad could happen."

"Are you scared, Alex?" Mary asked. I fidgeted with my fork in my salad.

"I'm just worried for you. If you go poking around on your own, you could wind up in a bad situation."

"Oh, my hero. I feel so much better knowing I have such a brave knight looking out for me. Thank you, Sir Jerks-a-lot."

"There's no need to mock me. I'm serious. For we all we know, he could be a killer, or, with how weird everything is, he might even be a ghost or something."

"You believe in ghosts?"

"Well, not really, but the idea has crossed my mind. Look, that's not important. I just don't think you should keep up this investigation. It doesn't seem safe."

"Well, you'll just have to come with me and keep me safe on my quest, brave knight."

"That's not funny," I sighed. "You're really going to go through with this aren't you? How about this, then? We wait for official information from the school until Friday. If we don't hear anything I'll...I'll go back to Powell with you for another look around."

"I can live with that," Mary said, smiling. "Anything to have my noble warrior at my side."

I groaned and returned to eating my lunch. To my surprise, she stayed at the table. The smile had faded from her face. We sat in silence for a minute. When Mary spoke again, the tone in her voice had changed. "Alex, do you really believe in ghosts?"

We spent the rest of lunch talking together, about ghosts at first, and then about ourselves since we didn't really know all that much about each other. I learned that she's a criminal justice student and wants to become a police investigator. That explained a lot. Still, I was interested to see her so certain of her future while I was just stumbling my way through. She stopped referring to me as her knight and even apologized for calling me a jerk all the time. Our time together was surprisingly pleasant. We conversed for so long that I was almost late to my first class of the afternoon. We shared a rushed farewell and parted ways, but not before promising to continue our conversation later. When I could spare a few seconds, I would send her a quick text with a relevant comment. She did the same.

We ate together again at dinner. I didn't even look at my friends' table. Our conversation continued, and we didn't talk about the dead student or our search for answers at all. Throughout the rest of the week, our interactions continued like that. We even hung out in her room Thursday night, where I found out she is very interested in old black-and-white movies. We watched one together, giving no regard for what time it was. I had almost forgotten about my promise to visit Powell again, but the following morning I woke up to a text from her: "Still no email. Powell at 8pm again?"

* * *

"I can't believe it's open," I told Mary. We were standing at the third-floor entrance to Powell. When we met at the King

Alfred statue, we decided to try to enter the building. The doors at the other entrances all refused us, but now we stood in front of an open door. We looked at each other in disbelief. I shivered in the cold. "Well, let's get inside before I freeze my ass off."

Mary pulled out her flashlight and lit the way. The darkness and the silence were quite eerie. The third floor looked as ordinary as ever, with one exception: there was police tape covering the entrance to the elevator. I didn't remember seeing it the other night.

"We should check the elevator doors on the other floors too. Maybe something happened in the actual elevator?" Mary suggested. I nodded, and we backtracked to the stairs. Two short walks later, we found the same tape on the elevator doors for the other two floors. We stood together on the first floor near the mailroom and the entrance to the elevator. "Okay, so I think it's pretty safe to say that whatever happened involved the elevator," Mary declared. "Did you notice anything different anywhere else? Because I didn't."

"No, everything else looks normal. But what could have happened? And why was that man using the elevator if it was involved in the death?" I walked closer to the elevator and examined the door closely. It didn't appear to be damaged. In fact, there didn't seem to be anything amiss about it at all. I looked at the call button. I felt compelled to press it. In the darkness, I reached out my hand for the button. I was about to touch it when, upon hearing a strange buzzing noise, I froze.

"Sorry, sorry, it's my phone," Mary said, retrieving it from her pocket. My body relaxed and I rejoined Mary away from the elevator, the compulsion to call the elevator gone. She was looking at her phone to find the cause of the buzzing. "It's an email," she said. She looked at her phone more closely. "It's an email from the president!"

"What does it say?" I asked.

"Oh god. It's about the accident."

"Does it say who it was?"

"Some worker at Powell. He was closing up for the night when the elevator failed with him inside of it. He died in the fall," Mary said. "Apparently, he was a new hire too. That's really unfortunate… and ordinary."

"Are you disappointed? Did you want there to be some conspiracy?" Mary ignored me as she continued speaking.

"Although that doesn't explain the man we saw in the window, or how he was in the elevator if it's broken. And that light was weird. Wonder what the cause of that—"

Mary's words were interrupted by a noise. It was a quiet, ordinary noise, but it made my entire body tense. It made Mary's face turn white with terror. It was the sound of an elevator ding. The sound an elevator makes when it reaches the desired floor. We both turned slowly towards the direction of the noise. From where we were, we could see only the recess in the wall where the door to the elevator resided. What felt like an eternity passed. Then, the hallway filled with light as the elevator door opened. The light cast a shadow. The caution tape over the entrance rippled as if a gust of wind had blown past it. I thought back to the last time the elevator door was open, to my subsequent nightmares.

"Did you press the call button?" Mary asked. She reached for my hand. "I saw you moving towards it."

"No, I swear. I didn't touch anything."

Mary's grip tightened. "Do you think it's him?"

The shadow shifted, and the caution tape ripped away from the wall. I took a step backwards, pulling Mary closer to me. At first a foot became visible, then an entire man. He turned his head to look at us. It was the man from the window. There was a slight glow to his appearance. Upon seeing us, his face contorted into a scowl. I felt Mary tug on my arm slightly, trying to back away from the man. For some reason, I couldn't move. I was rooted to the spot. The man turned his entire body towards us.

"Alex? We should go," Mary whispered from behind me, pulling at me again. I didn't respond. I just stared at the man. "Alex, please, let's get away from here."

Every muscle in my body screamed for me to run away, but I couldn't tear my eyes away from the man. I tried to speak, move, do anything, but I just stood still, staring. It felt as if I had been standing there for hours, but it was probably only a few seconds.

The man opened his mouth. "What are you doing here?" he growled.

His speech broke whatever spell had come over me. I screamed and started to run away. I pulled Mary along with me and tried to push my way out through the front doors. They wouldn't budge. I didn't even know these doors could lock from the inside. I turned around and saw the man walking towards us. I glanced at the stairs.

"We can get out this way! Follow me!" I shouted. Or at least I thought I did. Mary didn't answer me but she didn't resist the direction I was going. We started to climb the stairs. I reached the top of the first flight when I felt Mary falter. I must have been moving too quickly for her. She grunted as she stumbled. Her hand slipped out of mine.

I heard her scream. I heard her fall. Then I heard nothing.

I kept running.

* * *

The cause of her death was never publicly released.

No one except for me knew why Mary was in Powell, or how she even got in to the building when all of the doors were found to be locked in the morning. Her phone must have been broken in the fall, since no one ever asked me about her. I deleted her number and all of our conversations from my phone. I hesitated at her last message.

"Thanks for not bailing on me. See you tonight."

My throat burned as I deleted it. I called my parents and told them I didn't feel safe on campus with all the deaths. They agreed. I didn't tell them that I knew anything about either of the incidents, and they didn't ask questions. I spent the next two days in my room. I saw my roommate a few times, but we didn't talk. Then on Sunday, my parents picked me up and drove me home.

I never returned to Alfred after that, but every once in a while, I'd see a familiar flash of hair in a crowd that drew my mind back into Powell. Mary's scream would echo in my head and then, in an instant, the sensation would pass. One time, after I returned to the present, I couldn't find a trace of the hair or its owner. A chilling wind blew over me and very, very softly I could hear a voice, "Jerk."

MAN, YOU'RE ALREADY IN DEBT
AVA HAMEISTER

D URING MY FRESHMAN year of college, I had to walk back to my dorm late at night after my honors course on the opposite side of campus. There was a dark stretch between the last lamp on the path that ran along the Science Center, and the first street light in front of Tefft. On a cloudy night, the woods that approached the road were pure black. The dark never really bothered me, but that night it did.

It was late. I'd been busy. I was tired. Now that all my classes were finally over, I just wanted to get back to my room and go to sleep. Prior to this, I hadn't even noticed the dark hole in the leaves—that is, until it spoke to me.

"Hey, do you want a dollar?"

I didn't slow my pace at all, trying to hide my surprise. "No."

I glanced at the woods but couldn't see anyone. I was sure some kid was hiding in the dark, just to be obnoxious. But of course, better safe than sorry. I kept walking.

I avoided that path at night, and for the rest of the year, I forgot about the kid in the dark, until the end of the spring semester. Again, walking back late, the dark stretch loomed ahead.

"Hey, do you want a dollar?"

Really? I looked at the dark spot. "No."

"It's free."

"I really don't want your dollar." I was curious as to why this guy was, again, back out here in the dark. I kept walking.

He called after me, "If I came out there, could I give you the dollar?"

"No."

It was weird and creepy, but at least half of me found the encounter rather amusing, so later I brought it up when talking to some friends. They surprised me, saying that they had seen him too.

"It was a couple weeks ago! He offered us a dollar for a cupcake."

"A cupcake?" I asked.

She shrugged. "We were walking back from Ade and I dropped a cupcake I had and was like, eh, might as well leave it, and kept walking. Then, I looked back and there was this guy in the road looking at it. I said he could have it, just joking around, but he offered me a dollar in exchange. I said no, and he grabbed the cupcake and ran back into the woods."

I just shook my head. "That's so weird."

"You left out the weirdest part," my other friend said. He turned to me. "When he ran back into the woods, he did it on all fours, like an animal or something."

"That is weird. What did he look like?"

"We couldn't really see anything, just a vague silhouette."

So, the mystery of the cupcake-stealing, dollar-offering, slightly-deranged guy remained.

The next few years I didn't have to walk by that dark spot and forgot about him altogether. Then, one night as I was walking to Ade later than usual, I passed by that spot and felt a tingling on my neck. My hair stood on end.

"Hey, do you want a dollar?"

"Fuck off."

For some reason, he was still out here in the woods. Was he there every day? The next day I decided to walk by the same spot again.

"Hey, do you want a dollar?"

He sounded like he might be around the same age as me. "No."

"If I were you, I'd want the dollar."

"If you were me, you'd still have your dollar—it's yours."

I decided that that was enough for me and made it a point to stay away from those woods at night for the rest of my time at Alfred.

That was twenty-some years ago. Last night, I took my daughter to Alfred for a tour and a President's scholarship dinner. While the kids listened to some speeches, I decided to take a walk around campus to see what had changed. It was one of those dark nights with warm wind that felt like breath on your neck, but when I walked towards the end of the path, I felt a chill.

"Hey, do you want a dollar?"

I spun on my heel and stared at the darkest gap in the trees. My heart beat quickened, unnerved, but my stomach rolled with anger. This asshole was still here? I glared at the deep darkness framed by leaves and drew out my phone. I turned on the flashlight and shone it into the trees. The woods were empty. I spun around, looking for the owner of the voice. No one, not a soul. I approached the spot I always had assumed he had sat. I checked in the trees, even. No one.

Then, as my foot hit the grass, I heard the voice again. "So, you *do* want the dollar."

A LESSON IN BIOLOGY
AVA HAMEISTER

A FTER HE HAD graduated from our high school, Jared hadn't stopped bugging me to come visit his new school— Alfred University. I ended up in the area for a soccer game, so I finally gave in and stopped by to see him. The spring afternoon was already waning by the time I arrived. We started off with a decidedly interesting meal at Powell before he carted me off to see the campus.

Jared dragged me all over, showing me this and that. There was a pretty stone garden by a creek, a neat room in the library that was paneled in dark wood, a couple super-modern buildings that didn't fit with the rest of the old buildings, and way too many stairs and hills. The campus was pretty enough, but it was dead in the middle of nowhere. The populations of the two colleges on either side of the valley was greater than that of the one stoplight town between them—I checked.

"So, are there any ghosts?" I interrupted Jared's rambling about why internships were important, trying for a— hopefully—more intriguing subject.

"Um, yeah. I've heard of a few." He thought for a moment. "I don't put much stock in that stuff, but I've heard there's a little boy in Herrick, Abigail Allen in the castle, and there's a cow in the Brick."

"A cow?"

He shrugged. "Apparently they can't go down stairs."

I glanced up as we were walking past the castle. For a second, I thought I saw a pale woman at the window, but it was just a decorative rock.

We got lost in the art building for a long time. I'm not even sure why Jared tried to show me. It's not like he'll ever take an art class. We ended up coming out of a Glass Engineering building somehow. The sun had slunk below the horizon while we were inside.

Jared checked his watch. "Hey, do you mind if we head to the Science Center? I've got some bacteria to check on."

"Yeah, that's fine." My feet could use a rest.

As we crossed the street, heading for the looming brick structure, Jared had some more fun facts. "There's actually an entrance on each floor. See there in the corner? That's the first floor. Then over there's the door to the second..."

I tuned him out and glanced up at the pine trees. They were practically caked with crows, cawing and generally making a racket. They took off as a huge mass. They sounded like a wave crashing through a forest. It was murder on the ears.

"...And there's a skeleton on the third floor as well." Jared was still talking.

"Like, an actual human skeleton?"

"Yep. Oh! It's not the same one, but there's a ghost story about another skeleton. She was convicted of murder or something, and the university president offered her money for her skeleton once she died, and she agreed. Students kept stealing her though, and it pissed off her ghost. Now it's lost."

"I'd be pissed too."

We entered the Science Center on the second floor and went up one level. The stairs said Environmental Studies, but Jared said it was the Biology floor. Something about the stairs threw me off a little, so when Jared opened the door to the floor, I wasn't quite sure which way was which.

"Ah!" Jared led me to the left. "This is the room with the skeleton...and it's usually locked." He looked a little concerned as he paused, looking at the open door.

I stuck my head in. I found my stare matched by a thousand glass eyes. Taxidermied animals lined the room. Birds galore, millions of mammals. There was even a little, smushed tuxedo house cat. I wandered around, marveling at the collection. It wasn't that the taxidermy was good. No, most were falling apart or looked like they had just been pulled out of the dryer after a week, but there were just so many things. I paused at a shelf labelled "Fragile—Do Not Touch" and inspected a decaying great blue heron. The skin sagged off the bones of its legs; the feathers were matted and had been eaten away into spikes. I remembered the heron I'd seen that summer, dead and hanging from its neck in a tree, fifty feet above a pond, how its flesh had hung in strips off it. A ragged scarecrow.

I turned to Jared who hovered nervously at the doorway.

"Which is the human skeleton?" There were three around the room.

"Um, this door is usually locked. I don't think we should be in here."

"I'm not going to break anything. Which is it?" I asked again, approaching the nearest one.

He stepped into the room like he was breaking a thousand laws. "I'm not sure. I'd guess that one though." He pointed to one near the front, which was more tan than the white of the other two.

I looked at it. The bones had little porous areas here and there. Where the skull was cut, it was far thicker than the others. It certainly seemed real to my untrained eye. It was short—It? He? She? Oh well. I looked at the skull that had held a brain, eyes, a face. That person was gone entirely, reduced to the barest structure. I suddenly realized that I myself had a structure like this inside me. It was a strange thought.

"Okay," I said. "Let's go deal with your bacteria."

The building was a square, and Jared's lab was exactly opposite the one with the skeleton. He started to deposit his stuff on a table outside the door. He stopped and stared at my legs.

"Um, Jared?" I asked.

"I've just realized—you can't come in. You've got to have pants."

I looked down at my shorts. "Ah, okay."

"Here." He led me down to a door in the middle of the hall. Inside were some computers and tables and couches. "This is the bio lounge. Just chill here, I guess. I'll come get you when I'm done."

He disappeared back the way we'd come, and I flopped onto a couch in the corner, glad to be off my feet. I pulled out my phone, but it was dead.

* * *

I think I drifted off because next thing I knew I was opening my eyes and aching all over. The overhead lights were off. Someone must've stopped by to turn them off and not seen me. I tried my phone again, hoping for a flashlight, but it was definitely still dead.

I felt for the door. Finding the switch, I flipped the lights back on. The suddenness burned my eyes, and maybe that's what left the stark outline of a woman in my vision. It was just a split second, but I was fairly sure. I rubbed my eyes, blinked, flicked the lights on and off again. Nothing. Whatever.

I opened the door back to the hall. Whoever had turned off the lights had closed it too. In fact, all the doors in the hall were closed. I wandered down the hall. The door I thought was the lab Jared was in was also closed and locked. Maybe it was the other side of the building. I did a circle, trying different doors. All locked. Then it struck me; where had I come in? I did another lap, remembering a glass door that led to a sitting area and the outside. It wasn't there. It was all just awful tan and brown tile. Didn't Jared say there was an entrance on every floor? I did a lap again. Where was the table where Jared had set his stuff? Where was the room with the couches? It was all starting to look the same: locked doors, brown tiles.

I found the door to the stairs. We'd come up one floor, and the door outside was right where the stairs let out. As my foot hit the first step, something clattered. Was that the stairs? It didn't seem quite metallic enough. I applied my weight again. No sound. I hurried down the stairs.

The door on the next floor was closed too. Had there been a door here before? I pushed through and found myself face to face with more tan tiles. Was I on the wrong side of the building? I ran down the hall and around the corner. On the side that should have been the exit were more doors. More doors. Locked. I stopped. I needed to think. Which floor was I on? The stairs didn't help—only flecks of black remained to indicate the floor numbers.

Something clattered again. It definitely wasn't the stairs. I glanced around. Was I alone? Was there someone who could tell me where to get out? I looked down one hall. Empty. I hurried to the other side as I heard something gently clicking on the tile. Before I could get to the corner, I froze. My heart was still. The skeleton, the short little skeleton stepped around the wall. But was it the skeleton? There was a faint, blue-white haze. As I stared, it seemed to condense, forming a body around the bones, the skin hanging off like the heron's.

Nope.

I tore my eyes away and dove back into the stairwell. Back up. One floor. Two floors. Three floors? I was panting.

"I'm going crazy." I shook my head, patted my cheeks. This floor had to have an exit—an exit on every floor my ass. I took some calming breaths as I walked around the square building again. Nothing different, nothing unique. No tables, no posters, no windows—only locked doors. Was I in the basement or something?

Clattering. My head spun from whiplash as I found myself back in the stairwell. I didn't know I could move that fast. I climbed up more stairs, my legs burning. How many floors had I come up? Five? There were not this many floors in this building. I tried to look down to see where I was, but the switchback stairs blocked the bottom from my view. Looking up I couldn't see much more. Looking back down I saw a ghostly face looking back up at me.

I have to admit, I screamed. I ran out of the stairwell. Around to the other. Back down some floors. Where was I going? Everything was the same. Brown tile. Locked doors. Clicking. Stairs. Blue-white mist. I ran around, down, around, up. It didn't matter. I could hear her behind me.

I hadn't hurt her! I hadn't even touched her! I'd just wanted to see. Panting, I collapsed to my knees. My vision swam. I couldn't keep going.

The clacking. The clattering. The mist rolled around my feet and I froze.

There was a sudden impact on my shoulder. A warm, living hand?

"Jesus, girl. You can run."

I turned, falling back. It was a woman in a uniform. Alfred Fire Department. "What?" I croaked.

She wore a respirator or something. "There's a gas leak. You need to come with me."

Suddenly, the vaguely sulfuric smell registered. I'd assumed it was the building, but it was some kind of gas, like what they use with Bunsen burners.

But that gas didn't cause hallucinations, did it?

Waste Not
Allen Grove

I HAD A HARD time seeing the shoulder through the crazed windshield. Well, what was left of the windshield. The deer took out half of it. When I turned on the dome light I knew that CanMan was dead. The deer's twisted head lay where CanMan's face used to be.

So much for my good deed. Every Tuesday, trash day, CanMan walks into town to go through folks' recycling bins. And every Tuesday evening he carries a couple of big bags full of returnables back to the little hunters' cabin where he lives. I was driving to a friend's house out in the country when I saw CanMan lugging those bags through the drizzle. I thought I was being neighborly when I offered a ride. Shit.

The deer seemed to be looking at me. It was a buck, although only part of one antler remained. Its eyes were wide with death. I had the feeling CanMan was staring at me through the mangled creature.

I struggled to keep dinner down. I had to get out of the car. Shit shit shit shit shit. Breathe. I needed to breathe.

And I needed help. The signal strength on my cell phone blinked between one and no bars. I dialed 911 and hoped for the best.

"911. What's your emergency?"

"I need the police. I hit a deer. CanMan is dead."

"I'm sorry, sir. Bad connection. You hit a deer? Was your vehicle disabled, sir?"

"CanMan is dead! Why are you asking about my car?"

"I'm sorry, sir. Did you say someone has died?"

"The deer hit him. He's dead."

"The deer attacked him?"

"He was in my car. I hit the deer. CanMan is dead."

"Sir, are you sure he isn't unconscious? Please check and see if he's breathing, if his chest is moving."

I looked in the car and I knew CanMan couldn't be breathing. He had no face.

"He's dead."

"And what did you say his name was?"

"CanMan. You know, the can guy. I don't know his real name."

"Where are you sir?"

I gave her directions.

"I've radioed help, sir, but they're on a call over in the Hollow. It might take twenty minutes. Please stay on the line. I can talk you through CPR for Mr. Cannon."

I hung up. CPR would be about as useful as pissing on a house fire.

Within seconds headlights appeared over the hill. I prayed it was the police, but I knew it was too soon.

An old pickup, more rust than metal, slowed down and pulled in front of my car. The driver, a man who was as old and rusty as his truck, got out and walked back to me. He looked at the deer's ass protruding from the windshield and put his hand on it.

"Warm," he said. "You just hit 'em?"

"I killed CanMan," I said.

The man walked around to the passenger door and looked in. He shook his head. "That the squatter from up the road?"

"Yeah. It's CanMan."

"That's a buck," he says.

"Yeah. I know."

"You gonna keep it?"

"Huh? God no. That's disgusting."

"I'll take 'em," he says.

"Jesus. No. I have to wait for the police."

"It's best to drain 'em right away or the meat goes bad."

I felt like puking. I sat down next to the car with my head between my knees. The old man saw dinner hanging out of my windshield, and he wasn't going to miss an opportunity. I felt too ill to stop him. And what did it matter anyway?

He struggled with the big animal. I could hear him grunting and pulling. I'm sure the animal weighed more than he did. He opened the passenger side door to dislodge the thing. I just closed my eyes and tried to calm my stomach. The old man must have tied a rope around the deer's legs to pull the thing free with his truck. I could hear the remnants of the windshield falling apart and the hood buckling as his truck dragged the animal out. A bit more grunting and he had the creature up in the bed of his truck.

"Many thanks," he said, and then drove away.

A few minutes later, a police car and ambulance arrived.

The officer looked concerned. "Mister, are you okay? The dispatcher had a hard time hearing your call."

"It's CanMan. He's dead."

"Don't get up. Let the paramedics tend to you. Your face is cut up bad."

It was the first time I noticed that I had been injured. Blood was running down my face and dripping off my chin. My temple was throbbing.

The officer walked over to inspect my car with his Maglite. "Who's dead? Did you hit somebody?"

"I hit a deer. The deer killed CanMan."

"Who's CanMan?"

"You know, the can guy. He comes on Tuesdays."

"The deer must have run off. They do that sometimes. I've seen them damage cars worse than this and run off. They often die in the woods."

"No, the deer was dead too. Some guy took it."

I saw the officer whispering to a paramedic. He then turned to me.

"Mister, you've been injured. You have to go to the hospital for some tests and probably some stitches. It looks like you banged your head pretty good."

"What about CanMan?" I asked.

"Don't worry about him," said the officer. "Worry about getting your head fixed up."

As the paramedics helped me up onto the gurney, I looked over at the car. The dome light was still on. CanMan was gone.

"Where's CanMan? What did you do with him?" I must have sounded hysterical.

"Try to relax," one of the paramedics said. He looked like he was sixteen.

"Where's CanMan?"

My questions went unheeded as they wheeled me into the ambulance.

WHEN AND WHY ARE YOU?

SUSANNA BARGER

HAVING NO REASON to sit with them other than that they were familiar, I joined my six loose acquaintances around a rickety table for late night, fatty foods. Jimmy was tall and probably straight. Mike and Sara had known each other since kindergarten but were definitely not a couple. Abbi was the third best cheerleader on the squad, by her own report, and too scared of horses to take any equestrian classes. Bill was fat. I didn't know Karen.

We chatted a while and shoveled down french fries, but before nine-thirty even rolled around Karen set the tone. "You know, statistically, one of us is dead." Jimmy laughed but the rest of us only cocked our heads. Karen put her elbows on the table and leaned forward so far that her hair fell in her salsa.

"I'm serious," she leveled. "It's Halloween, I've only met three of you today, most of you guys don't really know each other, and none of us dress like we know what's up in this time period. In any kind of TV show, one of us would be a ghost."

"Which one?" Jimmy kept chuckling.

"Well, anyone I point out would just be random stereotyping. And they could lie about it. We need a majority consensus."

153

"Can you please take your hair out of your food? It's grossing me out," Abbi whined.

The conversation continued. Following the weird, but amusing train of thought, we decided to hold a conference of sorts and determine which of us was "actually" the ghost. We established four basic rules for the discussion:

1. Alive until proven dead.
2. The living could defend each other, provided they believed the other was actually alive. If no one came to your defense, however, to avoid you automatically appearing dead, Jimmy would make you the best case possible.
3. A five-to-four minimum was required to determine if someone was a ghost.
4. Multiple ghosts were not present.

The first round went quickly, with Abbi voted the ghost. She bore, in both name and appearance, an eerie resemblance to the wife of a past president's wife, Abigail Allen. Abbi had not known anything about Abigail Allen, and neither had Jimmy, so neither made a convincing rebuttal, and we ruled against her.

By ten o'clock we had purchased dessert, and despite Abbi's protests we started another round of ghost hunting. Bill had been on his phone most of the first session, so we looked to him to kick it off. He shuffled in his chair, adjusting a pin on his sweatshirt with his stubby fingers.

"This is stupid," he grumbled.

"Just fucking play along, Bill." Mike yawned as he grabbed another fry.

"No, this is stupid—"

"It's called imagination, Mr. Legend of Zelda. Give it a shot."

"Fine, whatever. Abbi's the ghost."

Abbi sat up in her chair, "Hey!"

"What?" Bill shrugged. "You were it last time."

"Just because I was it last time doesn't mean I'm it this time."

"Literally, I can make the same argument word for word as we did ten minutes ago, and boom, you're convicted. It's even more likely since you've got a prior accusation."

"That's not fair!"

"Hang on, hang on everyone." Jimmy waved his phone in the air revealing a page about the college's former presidents and their families on AU's website. Mike grabbed it and started reading. "There's a simple solution. Abbi, what would you say is your greatest activist priority?"

"What?"

"What cause do you want to most champion? You know, women's suffrage, the environment, poverty, getting lead paint out of kindergartens, I don't know, something like that."

"Uh, um," Abbi's eyes flicked around the table. "Probably the environment because, you know, like, global warming, and like, I had this stuffed polar bear as a kid and I'm not sure I want all the polar bears to die, and, uh—"

"Guys, you're making her nervous." Sara moved to stand up, but Mike waved her back into her seat.

"We've heard enough," he said. "From what the website is saying, seems Abigail Allen was pretty dead set on the whole women's suffrage thing."

"Bingo." Jimmy made finger guns at Mike and snatched his phone back. "And while a ghost might forget certain things about their past or might not know something about who they were supposed to have been, they definitely would not forget the passion that led them to be a supporter of one of the first fully coeducational schools in America. So, Abbi's in the clear."

Abbi celebrated by chugging her milkshake. But while Karen and Sara whispered to each other, and Bill checked his Instagram feed, she paused. And then slammed the half empty shake on the table, scattering strawberry globs into Karen's salsa.

"Hang on," she said. "If we've just presented damning evidence that I'm not the ghost this round, shouldn't that clear me from the last round too?"

"No." Mike finished the last of his fries. "That round's over and done, and we got you. We've just got more knowledge this time, so you're off the hook. But you're still the ghost from before."

"But if everyone knows they can, like, just google stuff to make a case, and I didn't before which is why I got busted, that means I got an unfair conviction."

"Whatever. It's done. You can move on now knowing you're not the ghost."

"But I wasn't the ghost before!" Abbi's voice was starting to break, and this time Sara did get up and comfort her.

"No one's really the ghost, Abbi. It's just a stupid game. One we should stop. Now." Sara glared around the table but dialed it up to eleven on Karen.

"It was just a game. No one said anyone here had to play." Karen shrugged. She was still picking tomato chunks from her split ends.

"Shame. I was having fun." Jimmy cracked his neck. "But I should be getting to bed anyway."

"You were having fun 'cause you got to be the good guy," Bill snapped.

"Whoa, hold up, what?"

"You got to save poor little Abbi when all us nasty accusers came calling. You got to be the good guy."

"Bill, drop it," Mike said as he came back from throwing his utensils away.

"You drop the alpha male thing Mike. You don't know me."

"Guys!" Karen barked. "Game's over. Bad idea. I realize that. We'll just go home, okay?"

"I think the fault," I began quietly, but seeing that none of them heard I cleared my throat and started louder. "I think the fault with our game's structure was that we left out the fact that any ghost here would logically know they were the ghost. And without that, they couldn't react with the standard guilt, or whatever, they would need to cover up their existence. Here." I pulled seven gum wrappers from my pocket, and with a sharpie drew a black dot in the middle of all but one. "The one without a dot is the ghost."

"I don't want to play," Abbi repeated, her head on Sara's shoulder.

"We haven't finished the round yet though," Mike mused, picking at some of his wispy chin hairs. "We've got to pick a ghost for this round, even if we just stop now. Abbi, if you quit, you're guilty."

"So what?"

"Well, you're guilty twice then. And a spoilsport, and kind of a brat if I'm being honest. Where's your sense of fun?"

"Mike, are you sure we should keep this up?" Karen took her gaze off her hair.

"They want to," Mike said, pointing his chin at me, Jimmy, and Bill. Jimmy and Bill made non-committal shrugging motions.

Jimmy yawned. "What could go wrong? Just another ten minutes. I never get to hang out with you, Karen."

We all looked at Abbi.

"Abbi," Mike started. "This only works if everyone plays."

"Just give me a fucking gum wrapper. And buy me a new shake. Then I'll play." Abbi stood up to use the bathroom.

Second round of deserts underway, the gum wrappers distributed and appropriately hidden, we knew one of us was lying about their identity. We added the rule that the gum wrapper could only be shown after the ghost was convicted, and we were a little less giggly than we had been the first time.

"So, first thing that needs to happen," Jimmy said, "Is we need to clear Abbi, so we don't repeat what happened ten minutes ago."

"What if we don't clear Abbi?" Bill murmured, glancing at a text from someone with an awful lot of hearts in their name.

"Forget Abbi." Karen leaned back while she sighed. "Finding who's guilty is more about behavior than anything at this point."

"What do you mean?"

"I mean it's no longer hypothetical, who looks like someone who died in the eighteen-stone-ages stuff. Someone here is not one of us. And they know it. We just have to process accordingly."

"Bill." The word was out of Mike's mouth before Karen even finished speaking.

"Aw, fuck you, Mike." Bill shoved his phone in his pocket. "Just because I'm not a string-bean or a roid-freak like the rest of you doesn't mean I'm the outsider. What's that campaign that's out? All bodies are beautiful?"

"I'm just saying you like to run your mouth. And you've been awfully quiet since the wrappers were handed out."

"It's called snapchat, shit brain."

"Bill," Sara interrupted. "You promised you'd be nice."

"You promised me he was just a friend."

"It's not your business who I date anymore. Remember that was your choice. And he is just a friend. So, fuck you."

It took a few minutes to calm the three of them down. It was still too early for most of us to either go home, or go to a party, and the majority were still curious about who the ghost was, so Karen suggested we go over to her dorm and finish over a couple beers. And everyone agreed, silently making up their mind to keep Mike and Bill on opposite sides of the room.

Karen's roommate went home for the weekend, so sprawling over piles of laundry, the separate beds, and two desk chairs, the group made small talk. Eventually though, the pull of the gum-wrapper question was too strong to ignore, and Jimmy broke first.

"All right," he said, stretching his arm over Karen's shoulder while he yawned. "I'll be the first to throw a stone. Sara."

"Wait, why?" Sara put her drink on the desk.

"You've been super nice to everyone. Like, all night."

"She's a nice person." Mike shrugged.

"I know that. But I also know people are less likely to go after someone that's been nice to them. She's playing us."

"She's good at that," Bill muttered.

"Bill!" Karen barked. "You know what, if you guys can't drop it, I'm going to grab a smoke. You coming?" She turned to me. I opened and closed my mouth a few times, then stood and followed her out of the room. Outside, Karen wasn't any calmer. I watched her exhale little clouds of cancer into the night sky, her face turning pink.

"I was just trying to make it up to Abbi," she muttered. "This whole second round thing. I felt bad about how the last game ended."

"I'm having fun."

"Yeah, well, just tell her I'm sorry, okay?"

"Why me?"

"You know her more than I do. Not sure about the rest."

I shook my head. "I met both of you today."

Karen stubbed her cigarette out on the dorm steps.

"Wait, really? Wonder who she's with then."

"Sara maybe?"

"Nah, Sara's just sensitive. She'd hug a porcupine if they needed it. But she's never told me about Abbi."

"We should go inside. It's cold."

"I like it out here."

"Uh, okay." I watched Karen walk out onto the grassy lawn nearby and stretch out beneath the clouds. I sat on the edge of the walkway, tucking my knees under me awkwardly.

"Maybe it's Jimmy? They seemed close."

There was no response. And then a dark chuckle. "Maybe she's the girl he's been talking about so much."

"You like him?"

"God, you're blunt."

"He doesn't like you?" I asked.

"Yeah."

"I'm sorry."

"Come sit out here."

"I'm cold."

"Come on, loosen up."

"You're kind of a lightweight, Karen." I stood up and dusted off my jeans. "Let's just go finish the game." She craned her neck to look at me.

"Sorry."

"You're fine. Just... have you told Jimmy?"

"Yeah. But I don't think he understands I don't just want to fuck anymore."

"I'm sorry." I waited for her to walk to me and gave her a quick pat on the back. "He's a jokester. They all are."

"I don't know about Abbi." Karen shrugged. "Let's go back inside." Something twinged in my gut, right under my belly button, as I watched her walk away from me.

Inside, Bill was bleeding. Sara and Mike were yelling at each other in the hallway. Jimmy had his hands over his face.

"What the hell happened?" Karen plopped down next to him.

Jimmy filled us in. "Oh, more drama. Bill thought he could pick a fight, got dinged pretty bad in the nose. Sara might just break up with Mike about it, even though she knows he had it coming. Spooked Abbi off."

"No RA's?"

"Your neighbor's getting one as we speak. I hid the beer."

"Brilliant."

All three of us slouched glumly on the bed. Eventually, Karen prodded Jimmy with her foot.

"You should text Abbi. Tell her I'm sorry about how tonight turned out."

"I don't have her number."

"Didn't she come with you? You're always talking about—"

Jimmy waved his hand dismissively. "Not a chance. I met her at dinner with you guys."

"Wait, what the hell." Karen sat up. "Bill's never met her, 'cause I introduced them. Sara introduced me to Abbi but said Mike met her first. Mike asked her for her number and her last name when we were eating, and asked how she knew Sara, and you two," she waved her finger at both of us, "have no clue either."

"I thought—" I started.

"Give me a minute." Karen hopped off the bed and ran into the hallway. We heard her yell at Mike and Sara to "shut the fuck up, do you want me to get into trouble?" But she was ignored. Five-ish minutes passed.

When she returned, her face had gone from red to white. She opened her hand and showed us a blank gum wrapper.

"You were the ghost?" I said.

"No, mine's in my pocket. I found it outside, in a couple of footprints heading out over the lawn. But the footprints just kind of… stopped."

"Leave the jokes to Jimmy." I rolled my eyes.

"I'm serious as the grave." Her hand was shaking a little.

The rest of the night was a bore, everyone going their separate ways either tired or angry. Karen had a hard time letting it go though. She'd brought up the gum wrapper from time to time, when she finished crying to me about Jimmy.

"But have any of us seen Abbi?" she pressed, wiping her nose on her shirtsleeve. I shrugged and wondered if maybe this would be the time she let me stay the night. Even if it was just on her floor.

Personally, I didn't know. I think Jimmy was tall, and probably straight given what he did with Karen between girlfriends. Mike and Sara had known each other since kindergarten, but were definitely not a couple anymore. Bill ate instead of talking to people. I didn't know what to do about Karen. And I don't think Abbi, ghost or not, needed six more problems when none of us knew what we wanted from each other to begin with.

PIECES

SUSANNA BARGER

SOPHIE HARBIN WAS a quiet, clumsy girl. When the team captain, Pete, introduced me to her, she had a string of bruises up one arm from falling down the stairs. They'd been dating since high school, Pete told me, and Sophie could barely walk through a room without bumping into something. She was twitchy. She always sat on the edge of the bleachers at games, jiggling her knee up and down, biting her lip when it looked like we were going to lose. Not saying I watched her. She's too short for me. Plus, Pete got grouchy whenever I tried to make eye contact with her. These are just the sort of things you can't help but notice. She was around Pete a lot. So was I. They didn't like being split up, Pete and Sophie. Wherever he went, she did too. When Sophie stopped showing up to classes, that's what I told Public Safety. And it's what I told the police a few days later when Sophie's parents reported her missing.

When a girl disappears, everyone blames the boyfriend, but Pete's not violent. I told them that. He'd walk through fire for anyone on the team. He's the best captain I've had in my two years of college playing, and he loved Sophie to death. He told her all the time. He's not violent. You can't take what

163

Miranda Shilling says for granted. I told the police that too. Miranda and Pete broke up on bad terms, way long ago, before he got with Sophie, and it's only bad luck she ended up Sophie's roommate. Miranda's a lying bitch. Maybe the word's strong, but I call 'em like I see 'em.

Hell, I admit Pete and Sophie squabbled. I never claimed they were couple of the year or anything. At the Halloween party before break they even got into a full-blown fight. And I admit Pete was in the wrong that time. Sophie only smiled at the guy in the Baywatch costume. But she was drunk, and she was egging Pete on. If not for that, Dean, our fullback, wouldn't have had to intervene like he did. I told the police that too. I'm an honest guy. And because of it, I won't let Miranda Shilling throw the kind of shade she's throwing when everyone knows how good Pete was to his girl.

It's funny, I can see my dad's stubbornness rubbing off on me there. Whenever he's not sure what to do, he sits me down at our kitchen table, folds one thumb over the other, and says "James, this I believe with the utmost certainty," in such a way I can watch the hairs he missed shaving wobble on both chins. Then he'll go on to tell me something about life. Or, usually, he tells me about women. I don't remember all the talks we've had, but I remember the one from when my mom ran off. I'll spare you the sob story. My father's one of those John Wayne types, born about sixty years too late to do anything but tell their sons the real man's way to live. Anyway, I've picked up the habit of making "I believes" at a crossroads. I'm not sure what to do with what's been going on the last couple weeks, but everything I've said about Pete, I believe with the utmost certainty.

* * *

On Wednesday night, three weeks ago, I helped Pete carry his laundry hampers downstairs in Bartlett Hall. He's a big guy, but he always waits so long to do laundry he has three hampers full by the time he finally gets around to it, and he needs a hand. He didn't have to pay me, but when we were done he gave me money for takeout anyway. Pete knows I'm a sucker for crappy Asian food. Later that night, while I was walking back from the Chinese place, I saw him hanging out by the bridge across from the ceramics museum on campus. He was dangling his hands off the edge, staring into the black water seething underneath. I watched his breath make clouds in the snowy air, clouds that got battered to bits by the wind before he spoke.

"James, I think you're my best friend," he said. He wouldn't look at me.

"You too, buddy," I patted him on the back. "You okay? Your face is getting red."

"Dean keeps a bottle of Beam in the plastic box under his bed."

"You guys did shots on a Wednesday?"

"Party don't stop, man," he said. Then he threw up on my shoes. I got him home and into bed so he could make the 11:20 marketing course he and Sophie had together. That was the first class Sophie didn't show up for.

* * *

That Friday, Dean said he didn't know anything about any Beam. I figured he was just hoarding it for a special occasion, something secret. I would have forgotten that Friday entirely, if not for when I was walking back from a party on Ford Street. I passed Bartlett on the way to my dorm, and I saw a red light floating in a fourth-floor window. Sophie'd already been missing for two days, it's all anyone was talking about, but when I looked up at the light in Bartlett, she was there. I didn't see a face, or her clothes, or anything really. I only saw the wispy brown hair, clumped around hunched shoulders, and I knew it was her. I pretended to be too drunk to get my keys out of my pockets, and someone let me inside.

Miranda Shilling opened the door I pounded on. I almost hit her in the face, mid knock. She was tall, but pudgy, with wild ginger hair and a nose so sharp it looked like it wanted to cut you. Her whole room glowed red.

"Where's Sophie?" I asked.

"What?" Miranda crossed her arms and leaned against the doorframe.

"I saw Sophie."

"Where?"

"Don't give me that. Why's she hiding from Pete?"

"Maybe because he's a violent, drunk asshole. Now where did you see Sophie? Everyone's worried sick about her."

"You're a liar. Let me in."

"James Tanner, you reek. I'm calling an RA." She began to slam the door, but I jammed my foot in the gap and pushed her aside. A red neon sign sat on her desk. It made me want to puke. Miranda's side of the room was neat, clothes folded, bed made. A glance at Sophie's side showed something like what they play on TV after a Texas town gets its ass kicked by a tornado. The clothes were all over the place, the covers tossed off the bed, and her chair was upside down. I could see dust beginning to settle on everything.

"Never mind." I grumbled. I'm not sure Miranda heard me over what she was screaming.

The guys downstairs managed to help me convince Public Safety that I was just drunk, looking for my friend's lost girl-friend because I was concerned. I didn't hurt anything or anyone, and Miranda couldn't lie over the voices of me and eight other guys, so she didn't press further.

* * *

That weekend, and the rest of the week, were pretty quiet, except I kept seeing Sophie. It was never her face, just the back of her head in the crowd, or one of her hands tapping on a window sill. I always knew it was her though. I didn't talk to Pete about it. I didn't talk to anyone about it. It was nuts. Maybe Sophie had never left the school after all and was just staying hidden somehow. I couldn't think of why. Maybe her grades were getting bad and she wanted an excuse to not fail this semester. I'd fake a kidnapping if it kept me from failing history. It was a stupid theory, but a bad theory was better than no theory at all.

Whatever the case, I was on my own. Even if I wanted to talk, Pete made it clear Sophie's absence was a no-go subject. The team knew he had to be hurting, but in Pete's words, "Bitches cry about their feelings. You want to make me your bitch, Tanner? You perv."

Last week Pete, me, and a few of the guys were sitting around the couches in Bartlett's common room after dark. I glanced by the flier on the window telling us to keep it shut or else bats would get in and give us all rabies and then we'd eat ourselves and die or something. Two sunken eyes pressed against the glass under the paper. Brown eyes but frosted over so they looked blue.

I jumped up. The guys' chatter stopped.

"Tanner, the fuck?" Dean stood up.

"At the window," I stammered, putting my back to the pool table and leaning on it to hide my shaking. Pete glanced around confused.

"You see a spider or something?" Dean pushed again. Four or five of the guys were looking at the window, looking right at the eyes. No, they were looking where Sophie's eyes bore through the glass. They were looking through them.

"Yeah. A spider." I let out a giggle pitched so high I might as well have been twelve.

"Fuckin' pussy. Any spider out there'd be frozen to death. You're scared of a dead spider." Pete spit, and everyone else roared.

* * *

After that night, Sophie kept getting closer. I'd walk to class and see her slumping against the corner of the art build-ing, her hair soaked and her skin tinged blue. I tried not to make eye contact. The day after that she'd be by the doorway of the bathroom, staring at me as I went to take a leak. No one else commented. No one else saw.

I accepted that I was crazy by the second or third time I saw her. I was having a nervous break, and I'd just have to go to a mental hospital over the summer and start popping schiz-oid pills in order to get better in time for preseason. Telling the guys wouldn't do any good; they'd just make fun of it. Couldn't tell anyone else cause they'd ship me off to the hospital right away. I didn't want to be the one to tell my dad I'd thrown out my perfect game attendance because I cracked and started seeing the captain's missing girlfriend. Don't get me wrong, people could tell something was up. I dropped eight pounds fast and kept getting smaller. You'd do that too if your mind up and shit itself, making you invent a ghost stalker. The thing that creeped me out more than the rest though? Sophie never talked. She leaned, she leered, she even put her blue-painted toenails right up on my desk (she was always barefoot), but she never talked while she was with me.

That was, until last Thursday, when she showed up in my dreams. I was walking to class and she was walking in front of me, backwards so she could stare at me the whole time. I screamed at her, ordered her to move, but she just marched on silently, her head cocked a little to the right. Finally, in tears, I begged her, "Just tell me what you want!"

She straightened her head, and in a hiss sounding like rushing water said, "I want you to see me."

* * *

I woke up drenched in an icy sweat. Somehow my window had sprung open and the room was ten degrees too cold. That dream kind of broke me, and I had to talk to Pete. I got up and went down the hall to Pete's single. He was slouched on a footstool, shirtless, polishing his great-granddaddy's Civil War sword. None of the RA's ever found where he hid it, but the guys would pass it around from time to time. The one rule was we had to be sober. One time Dean was boozing and gave himself a serious slice with the damn thing. The rule went in place the next day.

As I came in, I noticed a new coffee table in the middle of Pete's throw rug.

"Grab a seat, man." Pete jerked his head toward the fold out chair in the other corner.

"Table makes the room too small," I muttered while I sat.

"Spilled a coke a week or two ago. Huge goddamn stain right in the middle and my mom's coming up tomorrow. She'd pitch a fit if she saw."

"Ah."

My words got snagged in my throat. I coughed a little and tried a different question first. "What's the deal, dude?" I took a deep breath. "Pete, where's Sophie?"

Pete's hands stopped. "How should I know?"

"I dunno. But I think you do."

"Why's that?"

"I've been…"

"You okay?"

"I'm fine. I've been seeing things." My tongue tripped on the last bit.

"Things?" Pete put the sword down.

"Sophie. But she's super wet, and cold, and she's…uh… dead looking."

"Course she looks dead."

"What?" I spluttered

"She hasn't called me in more'n two weeks. Bitch better be dead."

"Pete, I'm serious."

"Hey, me too. Listen," he slid off the footstool and put a hand on my shoulder. There were old bruises healing on his knuckles. I hadn't noticed them before. "You're my friend, James, okay? My best fucking friend. I got your back, you got mine, and whatever these nightmares you've been having are, they're probably because you're worried about me. Because my girlfriend ran away or got herself kidnapped or sold into sex slavery in Guatemala or something. But look at me." He spread his arms for inspection, "Do I look like some damsel in distress? I'm handling it like a man. You do it too. Okay, buddy?"

He patted me on the back and I nodded. You can see, by how clear and how calm, and reassuring he was, that Pete's got only my best interest at heart. No matter what Miranda Shilling says, or that one girl who started making bullshit accusations last semester, or that flake who quit the team last year; no matter what they say, he's a good friend. He's a good guy. This I believe with the utmost certainty. So yesterday, when they pulled a foot with blue-painted toenails out of the creek by the ceramics museum, and then, getting down under the ice, they started finding more body parts wrapped in what looked like three-week-old laundry, I really didn't know what to do.

PIPISTRELLO
SUSANNA BARGER

No one ever thought I was cute until maybe after they got through middle school. And even then, it was only the strange kids. I understand. But my watching, sneaking, eavesdropping, prying and spying is comfortable. It is comfortable to be hidden, to know you see the little secrets people hold close to their oily skins.

I see you, in the first floor of your dorm, you with your girlfriend, how you don't hold her the way you hold the girl two doors down. You run your fingers through your girlfriend's thick hair. I have dreams where I'm snagged in that hair. I had a dream just yesterday about it. In the dream I struggled against the rich, red strands choking me like perverted twizzlers. I try to wail, but my throat is full of hair. In the dream your girlfriend is screaming. She is trying to bat me away, but I am so small and in my panic, I dig deeper into what I know. I know your girlfriend's hair. And I wake, lonely, in the afternoon.

You don't go to your classes on time. I hear you tell your friends how your art history professor is "up your ass" about attendance. Watching, listening, I feel obligated to tell you that if you only left your room ten minutes earlier than everyone else, you will surely make the most of your college experience. It's how I manage to eat on time. Of course, you wouldn't listen to me. You haven't seen me. You don't watch in the dark like you do in the day. I squat in the pine by your window, smell marijuana drifting out from upstairs, and wait for you to let me in.

If you'd let me in, I bet we could be friends. I could be your secret, like the girl two doors down. You could cradle me, and stroke me, and kiss my face and I would love you more than both of them. I would be loyal. I wouldn't bring people home. I couldn't. They wouldn't understand me like you would. I see the books you read. You like animals. You would have to understand me. And then you'd listen. But only if you let me in. Let me in.

HEALTH AND WELLNESS
SUSANNA BARGER

I T'S NOT THE PILE of castaway bongs that spooks you; nor is it the feel of crumbling leaves, bird crap, and sodden floorboards squelching beneath your feet. It's the smell. By the look of the bongs no one has even been using South Hall recreationally in years. Yet the weed smell still lurks, heavy and rotten, like someone got high by setting fire to a charcoal pit. Compounding it, there's a smell of rodents that died in the walls, the aroma of rain-soaked wood slowly being chewed away by bugs, and the musk that settles when no one cracks a window for a generation or two. Sweet, sickly odors pig-piled on top of each other, making a nauseating symphony of stench.

How weird is it that you have to walk by a condemned graveyard of a building to get to the Wellness Center? They call South Hall a historic site, but it's historic in the way a tombstone is historic. You're basically just giving patients a preview of what's to come, like they aren't stressed out enough by whatever disease is running rampant through their bodies. It's the most twisted buy-one-get-one special I can imagine. Every flu treatment comes with a blatant reminder of your own mortality.

Within two minutes I threw up. I'd barely shimmied inside between two cracking window boards, but the odors, and the gut crushing silence of the place made my insides swivel and pour out my mouth. A bit of hard-boiled egg got caught in my nasal passage, and I had to suck, cough, and splutter till it followed the rest of my stomach contents. That didn't make the smell any better. When I finished, I heard laughing from my friends.

"Backing out?" Isaac called, the smug bastard.

"Never," my voice cracked. I cleared my throat. "Never!"

"See you in two hours!" The rest howled. Their footsteps clattered on the pavement as they headed back to their dorms. I thought I heard Casey barfing too, somewhere on my right.

I would do my two hours in South Hall, goddamn them.

Fighting another wave of nausea, I wobbled my way to the driest corner of the room I'd broken into, the corner where the bong pile slumped. I kicked it over, scattering a cluster of insects with too many legs. They skittered away and disappeared into cracks in the corner molding. Slumping onto the moist floorboards, I ignored the squishing sound the wall made when I rested the back of my head on it. I had settled in for the long haul.

Fifteen minutes dribbled by like piss from a catheter patient. I made the immediate future bearable by framing it so I only needed to stay in South Hall for seven more segments of fifteen minutes. Then I only needed to do six. Then five. The stench began to hit in waves. One second it was fine, but the next had it steamrolling back over me so my eyeballs curdled in my skull. Honestly though, it was probably the only thing keeping me awake for the first half hour.

To distract myself I watched a bug on the boards of the window I'd gotten in through. It was green and round, swollen close to bursting like a water balloon. The bug lay on the board, an engorged toe of a creature, unmoving. I knew it was alive because its antennas twitched. I wanted to pop it. It's weird, I know, but I'm one of those people who can't help but pop the zits that well up on their face. The barely audible squirt, and the feel of releasing pressure is a greasy form of satisfaction. I needed to pop that bug.

I watched it a few more minutes, ensuring it was too bloated to use its wings, and crept forward. The putrid puddle I made when I barfed was outlined by slatted moonlight. It made it easy to make sure not to stick my hands in it while I crawled to the window sill. The bug lay, full and plump, on the board. I took a deep breath.

Why wouldn't it move? Chasing ladybugs as a kid, I had learned killing was never this easy. Even those clumsy, lumbering bugs that a five-year-old could grind between their fingers, fought for their puny lives. They waddled like the wind as Crayola-scented, sugar-fueled death in the form of little boys and girls bore down on them from above. Even ladybugs had a will to live. But this bug, as it was stalked by an exhausted, buzzed college kid, planning on squeezing it between his thumbs so hard its insides would crack its bones and spill out through the gaps, this bug who so clearly knew I was after it, would not move.

I put the question aside. I placed fingers on either side of its firm, bubbled body. And I pushed until, with a pop, I had satisfied that ugly urge. It was only after I realized I had nothing to wipe my hands off on. I made do with my jeans and sidled back to my corner.

Stirring in my idle mind, I tapped away the seconds like I was at a keyboard, trying to write time into speeding up. Before my parents got me on sleeping drugs, all my nights were like this. I'd just be tapping away the hours I should have been sleeping. Then, even when one medication was working, my mom would make me change it. Zolpidem brands were too addictive. Zaleplon knocked me out quick but didn't keep me asleep. That other one made my histamine response go nuts. I can't even keep track of the cocktails I'm on these days. Eszopiclone's usually a good bet. That's what I tell the Wellness Center if they ask. Those ones have side effects too though. That's why I first thought that I was imagining the itch.

Only minutes after I popped the bug, my fingertips began to burn. I scratched them on my jeans, then with my fingernails, but no use. There was fire welling in my skin; thick, pus-like fire making jelly of my bones and locking up my knuckles. I watched the skin turn white, then yellow, then red.

Breathing heavily, trying to soothe my hands any way possible, I flashed my eyes around the room. I saw I was not alone. Huddled around the holes in the corner molding, right by a water stain on the ceiling, were the bugs from the bong pile. Only they were different. They were rounder. And they were red. I blinked my eyes open and shut, sucking on my fingers to try and cool them down while I confirmed the lanky, leggy insects I kicked earlier were now ladybugs the size of quarters. I screamed.

"Hey," a voice echoed from the ladybug corner, "you okay in there?" It sounded like a girl Isaac brought to the party—Mary, or maybe Marie.

I tried to stammer out a reply.

"Dude, he don't sound too good." Another voice bubbled from inside the cluster.

"Were you smoking at Jake's?" The ladybugs shuddered as they called. It was Isaac's voice this time.

"What do you care?" It was hard to talk while still trying to keep my hands wet. The itch was spreading to my wrists.

"Just wondering if you were okay. His stuff gets cut funny sometimes. Casey was in a weird spot earlier."

Casey wanted to go in South Hall tonight. He brought up the dare. A few of the ladybugs had his smile, dazed and dopey, while they wondered how long someone could stay inside this place. Another shiver ran through the ladybug cluster. They hurled more questions down at me.

"They're not answering." Mary's voice finally said. "Should we go in after them?"

"They'll come out in the morning."

"I don't know."

"You wanna get Public Safety involved?"

"Actually though... yeah. I got a bad feeling."

"Okay. We'll go up the street and make a call from Becca's landline."

The bug cluster in the corner pulsed. It was just enough movement to let you know it was still alive. I should have known there would be ghosts in South Hall. It would make sense if it was haunted. But haunted with the ghosts of the decades upon decades of bugs that crumbled to dust in it. The green bug had to have been one of them. It had cursed me, and its acidic guts were making me burn all the way up to my elbows. I had brought ghosts too though. I brought the ladybugs I smashed, and chewed up, and swallowed in a feverish childhood rage. The swollen ladybug hive hibernating in the corner above me. That was full of my ghosts.

The itching and the burning had climbed up my arms and gotten a stranglehold on my throat. It spread down my chest in a red-hot wave. I couldn't scratch it all. I threw myself on the ground and started thrashing against the squelching floorboards just to try and find some relief. It was all so wet I couldn't tell if I rolled in the barf puddles or not. My elbows, my knees, my head, I was soaking wet and I was on fire. Splinters lodged in my fingers as I clawed. My knees got so scraped up they bled. I couldn't care less.

I yelled out to Casey to try and help me. He didn't respond. The bugs that were smiling earlier scuttled down from the corner, and made the shape of his body on the floor. Ladybug Casey, passed out in a pool of his own puke. I had to put his head on its side so he wouldn't choke to death. It was his idea to come in here anyway. I had to take care of him. But I couldn't. I was on fire.

The burning stopped when a cloud went in front of the moon. But not because of that. It stopped because the tumors started. Itching gave way to swelling. As I lay panting on the floor, I watched toe sized lumps swim up from my bones till they hunkered just under my skin. They wiggled to the touch.

"Casey... Isaac...Mary...Becca..." I moaned, calling farther away each time. I was having trouble breathing. All I could think was my skin was full of ghosts.

The good thing was you don't have to pop ghosts. They pop themselves.

That's where the memories start to get too hazy. There are flashes, bugs pouring out of my bulging hair follicles, an axe coming through the window we entered by, and roaring of blue and red light. Something grabbed me tight while the ladybugs fluttered back to the floor and lay dead on their barf soaked backs. They were wearing Casey's hoodie. That's about all I've got. Trying to get anymore, it's like trying to eat mashed potatoes with a straw. The thoughts just don't flow.

I don't drink anymore. My mom changed my medication again. But you asked about Casey, and that's my answer. We should tear down South Hall.

THE BLOWFLY MAN

MARY J. RUTHERFORD

AMELIA HEMMICK WAS being followed. No, stalked. Amelia Hemmick was being stalked. She tried to tell herself that she'd known he was following her from the beginning, but she wasn't naive enough to think he would let himself be seen before he was ready. Something in her said he had been preparing, silently watching, for a very long time. Weeks. Months, maybe. Years? She hoped not. It had been creeping up on her for a while now, though: the feeling of something other stalking her. Preying on her sanity day by day. Of course, Amelia had always been inquisitive, looking for the monster in the dark, the ghosts in attic, and skeletons in the closet. It came with growing up in a sleepy college town, located in a not-particularly-memorable piece of New York.

And so that's what her mother told her when she said she had a bad feeling. "You've always been so dramatic," her mother had sighed, setting her gardening shears down. "Did you actually see anything, or is this another one of your fantasies?"

Amelia had no clue what kind of a person would fantasize about this feeling, but of course at the time she hadn't seen anything, so she was forced to agree with her mother. She supposed another word for "inquisitive" could be imaginative and thus, dramatic. But then, she did see something. Only a suspended view on the other side of a chain-link fence at the University's sporting fields and strobed by the game-day crowd in purple and gold. A man standing preternaturally still as the world sped by, wearing old and mismatched business attire; brown hat and vest, grey coat and slacks, and a dirty white shirt. "Dirtier," Amelia thought, "than any respectable professional business should allow." In his hand was a briefcase, but it looked wrong. Too oily and scaly for leather, but not snakeskin either. It shone, greenish and shifting, in the light. And he was staring directly at her. Slowly, he smiled, teeth an impossible mix of cracks, spaces, and needle points. A single fly crawled out from between a cracked tooth and twitched along his swollen gray lip. Horrified, she tore her gaze away, stomach heaving. When she looked back, he was gone.

Over the next week, she tried to tell herself she had imagined the whole thing, but something about it was so disgustingly wrong that she knew she'd never be able to remember anything other than exactly what had happened. So she told herself he'd been looking at someone else. Someone behind her. There had been a lot of people around, all wearing Alfred University purple and gold, looking like merchandise mannequins. This worked—just barely—for about two days. Then she saw him again. This time he was closer. Standing—no— waiting, on the other side of the windows looking in on the student art show her parents had dragged her to. He pointed a fat, purpled finger at her the way someone pointed to let you know, "Yes, you."

As he smiled, he held up the briefcase and shifted the pointing finger to the bag and nodded enthusiastically to some unasked question. His eyes seemed to say, "Look. Look at this!" like a dog that had brought its master back a toy. Something inside told her she was the toy rather than the owner in this scenario. What did that make the briefcase? It shifted in the light, twitched and crawled. With a retching gasp, she realized what the briefcase was made of—thousands of fat little blowflies wiggled and flapped, a living skin of insect bodies. A few maggots squirmed blindly up the man's arm and disappeared under the folds of his jacket, which appeared somehow even filthier than the first time she saw him.

"Oh, how cute, you've made a little friend." With a start, Amelia turned to her mother, who was looking at the Blowfly Man in that doting way all adults look at small children.

Amelia had no idea what her mom was seeing, but it was not the Blowfly Man. The man's bulging gray eyes met hers and the excitement now had something malevolent behind it. It said that he knew he had fooled Amelia's mother.

"Do you think he has a sibling that goes here?" her mother asked.

Amelia didn't bother answering. She walked away, hoping the man wouldn't follow, but knowing he would. He trailed her the rest of the day, and when she didn't see him, she could hear the flies. One or two at a time would circle around her, taunting her. It was like they could smell a decay that hadn't even started yet. Not on the outside, a part of her mocked. The part somehow sounded like she imagined the man would sound, if he chose to speak.

* * *

It was like that for the next week, her seeing him everywhere she went. His brown leather shoes on the other side of a bathroom stall door, an encounter ironic in what it did to her bladder. But that wasn't all. His shadow against the projector

183

in the movie theatre. His battered nails tapping an arrhythmic melody against her bedroom window at night like some sort of demented lullaby. And when she didn't see him, it was his flies. They'd crawl and buzz around her, rarely getting close enough for her to swat them out of the sky, but close enough still to fray her already worn nerves. One morning, she awoke to a particularly fat blowfly trying to work its way between her lips, its little legs prodding and twitching. She felt the ghost of it on her mouth the rest of the day, no matter how thoroughly she washed.

Amelia knew that something was coming, though no amount of internet searches could tell her what. He was getting closer with each passing day and the flies had become such a constant companion that even her absent-minded parents were beginning to notice. So when he appeared on one otherwise quiet night as soon as she turned off her lamp, she was unsurprised. Unsurprised, but no less terrified. She was sure he could hear her frantic heartbeat from the way his swollen lips twitched in the cruel ghost of a smile. Again, the man pointed eagerly to his briefcase. Today it looked less like a true briefcase and more like a vaguely square shaped swarm. And an angry sounding swarm at that.

"Ehn!" the man gurgled and shook the case at her. It took her a moment to realize he was saying "in." Maggots dropped from him in clumps before wriggling into the shadows below her bed.

She shook her head rapidly, feeling more and more like a rabbit caught in a trap. Her heart seemed to be trying to imitate the animal as well. The man frowned, almost confused, as if he did not understand why she was refusing him in all his horror. Again, a buzzing voice filled her head, teeth-grindingly horrible.

"Get in the case or get in the suit, girl."

Again, Amelia shook her head, mentally calculating the chances of her making it to the door before he could catch her. Impossible. His wide, sagging frame blocked her path entirely.

"Decide or we decide, girl." Both the case and the man's coat thudded against her duvet.

Decide, decide, decide— It was a chant in her head, almost enough on its own to drive a person mad. "What will happen to me?" she asked.

Amelia herself was not sure if she meant inside the coat or inside the case, but it didn't seem to matter, as neither the man nor his flies answered her. Some part of her already knew. The man was a swollen gray mass of decay, and that would be her fate too in his clothes—literally in his shoes. The case, however, was as big a mystery as death, perhaps even bigger in that she had no idea how much it would hurt. It was the shudder-inducing memory of the blowfly's legs scraping her teeth as she woke up that made her decision for her.

Amelia took the dirty coat and slipped her arms through while the man held it for her. The flies swarmed her and the man. They filled her ears, her nose, her lungs as she breathed until she was gagging on flies—and then they were gone. Back to the briefcase.

The Blowfly Girl raised her eyes to the moon shining through the window and smiled through her cracked teeth.